Beckon the Ravens

By Bradon Nave

For information, or to order additional copies, please contact:

Beacon Publishing Group
P.O. Box 41573 Charleston, S.C. 29423
800.817.8480| beaconpublishinggroup.com

Publisher's catalog available by request.

ISBN-13: 978-1-949472-03-5

ISBN-10: 1-949472-03-5

Published in 2020. New York, NY 10001.

First Edition. Printed in the USA.

For my mother, Connie

Rural Idaho, 1975

1.

Mostly dead. *Oh, how I can relate.* The large dogwood stands at the base of the dirt driveway. Tall and tattered by decades of extreme weather, all but a few branches are barren, without bark and unvarnished. *Mostly* dead, yet speckled with evidence of a strangled, thankless existence. Quite a cruel kinship we share. Of all the vegetation gawking my direction from outside the bedroom on this April morning, I feel most drawn to that awkward tree.

I'm never anxious to look there. Through a half-ripped screen tacked in a wooden frame, my gaze typically rests on the tree, or dingy tractor parts, dusted in snow or baking in a summer's oven, depending on the season.

But then there's spring. Spring holds a different paintbrush entirely. It paints a morning sky that could rival even the richest lilac. It dapples this plush country yard with all the colors of the Crayola box and leaves me grinning sleepily for the first few seconds after he bangs his alarm clock.

The smile fades. I could gulp every one of those

colors by the gallon and remain black inside. Black as night. Black as a raven's back.

He reaches for me. Words are useless now and so I'll resort to finding faces…countless faces within the rain-stained ceiling above us. I know for the next one to fifteen minutes, I am his, physically.

***

Creaking floors were once heartening. My childhood home moaned and grumbled with every step and offered a soothing reminder of the presence of others. Here…here the thumping of boots on aching, aged hardwoods, reminds me only that he has yet to depart to the fields for the day. Back and forth and all throughout the home until finally the spring of the screen-door stretches and then slams it violently closed. His truck whines and stutters and hesitates…as if it too had consumed an ungodly amount of whisky the evening prior.

A draped white sheet pulsates atop my breasts as I listen from the bed. My breath remains captive within me until the engine outside comes to life and I hear it wander away down the dusty driveway.

Silence. If there are birds or other living beings in or outside this stucco block of a home, I'm not hearing them now as I fill my chest with air—with his scent.

I should move. *Blink.* I should tear the bedding from my semen-smeared torso and fly from this mattress to wash away this musky advancement. Yet I am still.

Routine. The word once slid across my tongue as casually as iced tea. It now nauseates me from my core. Little more than a face in a photo frame, the girl who disintegrated and a way to begin his day, I find my existence has crumbled and I am at best a piece of a routine.

I move. I slide from the shambles, into the bathroom and the cast-iron tub.

The warming water disappears down a gurgling drain and into some abyss—perhaps a blue sea or the center of the earth. I imagine myself two inches tall and aquatic, circling a tiny, twisting waterway and emerging somewhere warm and safe. A sink, clad with beard trimmings and streaked with used toothpaste, reminds me there is no such escape route. There is no abyss, the drain ends where a rotting sewage-tank begins. *There is no escape.* Or rather, nothing to escape to. I came here with my husband.

Soaking, inhaling hot steam adorned with nothing more than the aroma of cheap bar soap, I find additional faces—mostly eyes peering down to me from the ceiling above. What judgment might such eyes cast on me if for but a moment they blinked? Would they glare or appear sympathetic?

There are four saucers and two glasses next to the kitchen sink that need put away. The sun is out; he'll expect the wash to be air-dried. If I'm vigilant, I may be done in time to meander to the edge of the woods and be at one with nature rather than my thoughts.

The kitchen is a cold box of green linoleum flooring, peeling upward in the corners, and little windows with atrociously mismatched drapery that overzealously protects outsiders from prying in. My duties here are complete in mere minutes. Basket in arms, I tote the wash out the backdoor and to the clothesline. There aren't many garments to hang and I'll tend to the sheets once I've returned from my jaunt and they've cycled.

Chores complete, I look past a dilapidated coop and

to the opening of the meadow. Appearing mysterious and all-encompassing, the woods may well entice the curiosity of visiting hands. It evokes only calmness from me, nothing wild. I've wandered worn trails and sat by cool streams and the countless hours have depleted any mythical quality the forest might have once had.

Within the forest's clutches, I'm at peace with the reality that I am anchored among everything I am not. Scampering ground dwellers and twig-hoppers far above…they feed upon a bountiful freedom and I'm left to briefly visit and taste its splendor. These are the scraps.

So plush and full and teeming with plenteous life. This is a stark difference from the scene I gazed upon only months prior. A forest can't be bashful once the winds of winter come howling, strips the trees and leaves it shivering in a nudity some call beauty. I call it ugly. I need this ugliness—*I crave it*. I long for the day the cold strips him of all he hides behind and under. I wish it'd expose him and leave him to quiver under accountability.

I won't enter today. Today I'll merely watch the squirrels and listen to the jays. The grass leading up to the mouth of the forest is a thick carpet rolled out for me…beckoning me…but entering today, with this frame of mind, would be no different than walking briskly from a high cliff's edge.

There is escape—nightshade, a moccasin's kiss, or a final swim in the spring-fed pond. Although not the escape one might assume appropriate for an otherwise healthy, nineteen-year-old woman, the woodland does offer many options, all leading to one glaring-red alternative. For now, I'll remain planted. I came here to be with nature and not to think of such things, even if I find comfort in them.

Something uncomfortable…anything but comforting. The grumbling of an approaching vehicle snares my attention, snapping my face sideways as my gaze lands on the single road leading from the home. My life and this house are nestled between the woodlands and the dead-end dirt road. Those traveling this road have either done so by accident or are returning to roost.

Loose, long hair obstructs my vision as I stand, clutching my nightgown. My face heats with anger. I request little, if anything. A short venture and an hour daily to refresh my lungs with clean air. *He's one million leeches.*

He's early…too early. Perhaps he's ill or injured. But then, the road, encompassed in overhanging willows and tall oaks on either side, echoes another idea. The vehicle approaching is not his. It groans and moans in a similar fashion, yet the variance is quite distinguishable.

A green farm truck, mildly rusted on the hood, finally appears on the drive. The dust and glaring sun choke out any visual of the approaching intruder through the windshield. I watch the vehicle cautiously, assuming the driver will return to where they came from. Much to my dismay, the wheels come to a crunching halt and the engine rests just where Leroy's truck would typically set.

I haven't the patience for such interruptions. These brief moments, fleeting as they are, I witness them being yanked away by a copper-skinned thief. The driver, a pepper-haired gentleman sporting a tightly tucked button up shirt, denim jeans, and boots, makes his way to the front door. Initially I remain stationary, hoping he's simply selling goods or has the wrong address.

When his polite knocks go unanswered, he returns to climb back inside, start the engine, and drive away. Only as he departs, dust diminishing and porch in view, do I notice the remnants. He's emptied two passengers—both of whom appear much younger than he and completely disheveled—from the vehicle. Entirely flabbergasted, I watch the vehicle casually traipsing away.

"Wait!" I nearly lose balance running toward the bewildering scene. The driver pays no mind to my objection and so my focus turns to the man and woman near the front of the home.

So prominent is my scowl that it is aching by the time I've reached the duo. Wide-eyed as two kittens in a hailstorm, they look at me as if I'm a banshee, storming toward them from the thicket. "May I help you?"

Spanish mumbling enters my ears as I approach. I'm equally irritated and perplexed. These two…it would appear as though someone snatched these beautiful specimens from the cover of some Central American travel magazine, rolled them in filth, and tossed them on the lawn.

"May I help you?" Softer, my tone coaxes a shy grin from the man, yet he says nothing. "Why are you here?"

"Please. Can you help us?" Her voice is a salty dark chocolate—smooth and soothing with sharpened undertones.

They're anything but kittens, and yet they're just as defenseless. Why have they been left here, at the mouth of my misery? I can offer nothing. I'm no savior.

"Help…help you? You must be here by mistake. You need to go—"

"Leroy? This is his home?"

He's summoned them. He's brought them here. *It's happening again.* I'm useless to stop it. "You're looking for Leroy?"

She nods gleefully.

What is there to do but show them in?

2.

Stagnant air invades my lungs, perfumed with a hint of rotting leaves and soil. Dewy and dappled with forest floor debris, my skin mounts an army of tiny goosepimples as the calls of some wild thing beleaguers my ears. Close. Too close.

Just beyond a crumbling log and midway up a large spruce is the blur of something brown, scattering in a clamorous commotion. From the chaos falls a silent casualty—a soft blue to the forest floor. Molten yellow spills from the beautiful capsule…an egg.

Among the branches above, an unruly display unfolds in flashes and odd callings—two beautiful onyx lovers surround a cradle-robbing fiend. Ravens.

The squirrel chatters and fusses about, perhaps pleading as it scurries in and out of the shadows. And then it's falling—twisting and reaching aimlessly, landing oddly among jagged things next to the shattered shell.

The first of the ravens is quickly upon what appears to be a weak and wounded varmint. I watch contently as justice is delivered in a hypnotic spectacle mere meters from my feet. Bashful beams of sunlight peer through the treetops to kiss the blackened back of the feathered executioner. The wee-one's cries for leniency only conjure the second of the birds. The duo work in sync to bloody the animal until the cries cease and they peck and peel a lifeless corpse. To witness death is an unforgettable experience. To behold retribution is invigorating and will remain ever chiseled on my brain.

As eyes and innards are plucked and gobbled, I find my cheeks are aching…aching under a curious smile as I watch the macabre mayhem from a healthy distance.

So elegant—their havoc. I crave their strength—the beauty within their allegiance.

Oh, to beckon the ravens. To watch as they descend on those who've maltreated me, leaving them sightless and hollow.

Their deed complete, they leave the ground for their home of twisted twigs, clutched in the treetops. "Don't...don't go...don't—"

"Go where? Please? Some more?" Her kind request parts my melancholy like wind through smoke. From the kitchen sink I turn to see the girl, Anna, nodding toward Q's plate.

I'm assuming Q is short for some other name but haven't found myself concerned enough to enquire. His eyes say so much while he says so little. His soul seems kind...potentially naïve. I harbor no hatred while dishing eggs and fried breakfast meats to the thankful. They're hungry and something about the way they consume their meals in a ravenous and primal manner pleases me. They're in need of substance. Unlike *him*...he'll slide piece after piece of grease-laden meat through his glistening red lips. Chewing and slurping resound all throughout the kitchen and are rivaled only by the ticking clock. *Him*...he'll arrive soon smelling of the field and last night's liquor.

These two, Anna and Q...I could cloak my thoughts in concern but for what cause? I can do nothing. I'm simply a forgotten living being and when I am dust, I will be a forgotten departed being. I could ignite dread within their souls. I could fling the door wide with wild eyes and demand they run for the woods before he returns. I could softly fill their minds to the brim with horrors. Horrors that would certainly have them fleeing voluntarily. *Where to* is the question. Certainly, they have nowhere to go. They have only the clothing on their backs…rags…and the desire for something *more*. They're perfect.

"Emily. When will Leroy be home?" She gently flicks a spot of egg from the corner of Q's mouth. She seems to adore him and stays at his side like a watchful lioness. So fierce and poised regardless of their predicament. I'm fond of her. My heart might break for her if it wasn't previously pulverized.

"Soon. Very soon." It's then a shimmer snares my gaze. A gorgeous feather, black with an oily purple overlay, adorns her mess of black hair, which falls unbound several inches past her shoulders.

She watches me curiously as I stroll barefoot to her for a closer examination. Upon inspection, I see only hair in need of washing and brushing…no feathers. It's been swallowed up. "Your feather. Where did you get…where did it go?"

"Pardon?" She scowls and smiles simultaneously.

"The feather in your hair."

A slight giggle and she's pulling her loose locks behind her shoulders. "Oh. Si. I need to wash. Please, can we use your bathroom?"

Lovely singing, running water, and an occasional baritone voice sound from behind the bathroom door. It's something refreshing to be in the presence of other humans…other than Leroy. To hear them doing what they do when mildly comfortable has tossed my feelings into an emotional inferno. When he arrives…what then? Perhaps not kittens, but if I stand by idly, then they're the sum of sacrificial lambs. My mind is racing, the minutes are dwindling, and I haven't the clarity to piece together something rational.

They make no effort to cover themselves as I fling open the creaky, white-painted bathroom door in a hasty fashion. They only grin, facing one another while sitting in the tub.

"You must dry off. Please hurry, you aren't safe here."

Droplets dive from their hair and faces—glancing, with curious expressions.

"Please! Don't be modest. We need to move." I march briskly to the towel closet as the couple stands from the milky-white water. Although I desperately attempt to maintain my focus forward, like a sunflower aching and turning for the sun's kiss, my sight is ensnared by the beauty of their nudity from the corner of my eye.

I leave them to dry and fetch them something to wear. Anna will fit nicely in one of my many cotton dresses. Finding fitting attire for Q might prove more difficult. When I return with clothing in hand, I'm bewildered to find them dressed in their original clothes. The clothing is wet, yet clean and presentable.

"I've brought you fresh clothes."

"Thank you. We are here to help you. Not to be a burden." Her soft reply comes with a kind smile.

"Indeed. Come, you are in danger. I can't explain now, but I'm stashing you in the smallest of the three barns. There is hay to sleep on and I'll bring provisions—"

"Danger?" Anna asks. Her expression is heavy with concern.

"Yes." I reach for her hand. "Danger. Leroy—"

"We are here to help you with him. To help—"

"I understand why you are here. You were lied to. Hired hands have shorter lives than motherless piglets on this farm. Everything you were told is a lie, but I haven't the time to explain right now. Please."

As she nods, fear darting through the darks of her eyes, I watch the last of the ivory water disappear down the rusted tub drain…and with it, the beautiful black feather is gulped away. "Oh! Your feather! It was so fetching." Shrugging, I nod toward the door. "I see them nearly every day on my walks. It will be no issue collecting you another. Let's go."

***

The world shifts as rubber on gravel has me pacing in the kitchen. He is home. A potato of a man exits the rusted toolbox of a truck with bottle in hand and makes his way toward the door.

Inside, every nerve within the skin of my back is immediately hypersensitive in anticipation of his repulsive touch. I stand facing the sink in hopes he'll retreat for the bedroom and nap the fading day away.

A migraine in a physical form…throbbing, nauseating with the ability to turn the air sour, he enters the home, hefty boots on linoleum, and lingers foul-breathed behind me.

"Meyrick." Agonizing as an eggshell shard shoved under a nail while cleaning, his voice assaults my ailing spirit as relentlessly as spring mosquitoes.

"Please…my name is Emily—"

"Hush with that shit." Muscles tighten as his hands work their way up my torso like colossal arachnids. "You cooked?"

Barley-ripe breath and whiskers wisp across my neck, eliciting a visceral response like that of smelling soured milk.

"I was hungry, Leroy. Please. The dishes need tending to."

"Tending to? Done, Meyrick…they need done." Low and cold, his words leave me frigid. There is no point in resisting. Doing so now might alarm him and leave him suspicious of my actions.

"You just left all this goddamned food sittin' in the sink? Wasteful as shit."

"Are…are you hungry, Leroy?"

"Starving." His grasp on either breast from behind is uncomfortably aggressive. "The bedroom, Meyrick."

"Yes. As soon as the dishes are washed."

"I won't say it twice."

***

Whisky-kissed air hangs uncirculated over a sawdust-covered floor. There are no windows to crack and the only door to the barn is large and remains closed. Scripture and flasks are passed about freely amongst my father, Samuel, and a few other gentlemen of the community.

Camaraderie among the group seems strangled with palpable tension. Laughter is laced in aggression; sighs are elongated and stinging sweat streams foreheads and dampens garments. There's nothing atypical painted here.

I stand far enough from the seated men so that I don't appear to be prying, or even concerned by their chatter, but close enough to fetch fresh glasses and ice when summoned. My childhood girlfriend, Jennet, is by my side. We giggle at innocent jokes whispered under our breath.

Still in our Sunday service gowns with our hands clasped behind our backs, remaining nearly motionless in the sweltering atmosphere and acting as errand-girls is the only way to escape a strict eight-thirty bedtime at the age of seventeen. Also, there's the possibility that I might see Kaleb.

"Meyrick, I feel he'll ask your father soon. I know it." Jennet's whisper has me biting my bottom lip and looking for observers.

"Jennet," I casually whisper—lips barely pried, "we mustn't talk of that here. Anywhere but here."

"Has he kissed your lips, Meyrick?"

"Jennet, be quiet." My pulse amplifies. Scanning the small audience shows no evidence our conversation has been overheard but I'm writhing within myself.

"Meyrick!"

"Coming, Father." I rush to him and his raised glass to fill it with fresh ice cubes.

"Meyrick!"

"I know, Father," I blurt out.

"What the fuck are you talkin' about?" Leroy barks.

"I...I beg your pardon?" I turn from the sink—dumbfounded.

"I swear on everything holy you get crazier every goddamned day."

With the day's end comes a mild reprieve. On a typical day Leroy consumes enough liquor to leave him as flaccid as a drenched quilt—snoring and fastened in place until his alarm sounds and has him riling and cursing through the home with swollen, screaming-red eyes.

Any evidence of a nauseating ravishing was scoured

away earlier in the bathroom and hastily disposed of.

Leroy has prepared a tall drink and is enjoying it at the kitchen table. The beads of sweat speckling his forehead rival those adorning the glass before him. Red cheeks and thickened eyelids give him an almost sunburned look. Sun-kissed perhaps, but this appearance, overall, stems from the inside. I do anticipate that one morning I might wake to find him poorly, wailing, and as yellow as a caged canary.

He pours another. The sooner he's inebriated and face down on the worn bedding the sooner I'll be creeping into the night to tend to kind strangers. There's something revitalizing associated with having a sense of purpose—to feel needed.

"Meyrick!" His belligerent snarl trips out his mouth.

"Yes…what is it, Leroy?" I approach with a heavy foot.

Like some bloated boar, his engorged face turns to me. "Meyrick…do you know the difference 'tween a dish…a dishrag, and a fuckrag?" he asks before belching.

"I'm unfamiliar with the latter term, Leroy—"

My wrist is snatched up in his drunken grasp as I stand just above him.

"Please, Leroy. You're hurting me."

So repulsive is his grin that I must focus on the thick black hair protruding from either nostril rather than it.

"A dishrag can be washed…made clean. You can scrub it and get all that grime and shit up out of it. A fuckrag," he chuckles—a snorting swine, as his watery gaze rests below my midriff, "well, a fuckrag is just a soiled piece of nothin'. No use 'cept what it's good for." His gaze meets mine once more. "Make sense?"

"That's cruel, Leroy."

Impressions from his grasp remain on my wrist after I'm released. He turns his focus to an empty glass.

"Here. I'll fetch you another."

The drink I pour is strong. Strong enough to have a common man or woman gagging and yet he's gulping it as if he's drinking freshly squeezed orange juice. I watch him stumble and stagger as he arises and makes his way to the bedroom. If not for the walls around him, he would fall flat. The bed springs creak and moan and within a minute he is snoring…and my eyes purge something sour from my core. My tears fall heavy to the floor below me, and if it were any other night I might teeter and topple and wail into my apron. Not tonight…tonight I have a purpose. Tonight, I must dry my tears and clear my mind. If only for tonight…for this brief period, I am something of substance to someone. If that isn't reason to compose myself then I'm not sure what is.

***

Milk, honey, and warm bread have them eagerly filling their cheeks and grinning. A small lantern gives just enough soft light to illuminate an impoverished scene with hay for bedding and yet there's a bountiful glee twirling about the atmosphere as physically as fireflies on a still June night. I've succumbed to the idea that these individuals aren't the annoyance I'd originally assumed. No, they are far more. I picture the two of them strolling carefree, hand-in-hand, only the tribulations of young life ahead of them…not those associated with the likes of Leroy.

I find myself longing to assist them beyond simply feeding them and tucking them in with field-mice and barn owls. I find I'm caring for their wellbeing, and to do such a thing may prove dangerous but I haven't much to lose.

I am no sanctuary…I am little more than remnants. However, where there is hope there may be some form of resolution. Perhaps that's what these two are…*hope*. Not hope for myself. I'm quite at ease with the idea of fading like a pale orchid to be forgotten by those who may have once fancied it…but hope for these beautiful and courageous people before me. They have yet to taste the horrors of this ugly place.

"Tell me, how are you here now?" I sit tastefully, knees touching, and hands clasped as if I'm attending a Sunday picnic. My question seems to have perplexed Anna. She boasts a puzzled grin and sets her bread aside.

"Here? How?"

I assure my smile and tone are equally warm and inviting. "Yes. Tell me your story. What brought you here to this place?"

A soft serenade of crooning crickets, toads, and other nightly creatures enhances the scene. We sit silently within the flickering light and dancing shadows—momentarily marinating in the enquiry.

"You. Ma'am. You told us to come here. We are here for you." There is a swelling conviction in her gaze, solidified under a hefty scowl of confusion.

"I…I understand Leroy summoned you as work hands, I'm asking something deeper. Tell me about you. Are the two of you married or do you plan—"

The soft light illuminates a brilliant smile. She giggles and takes Q's free hand. "Yes. Bonded. For all of ever. First comes the home, then comes the babies.

You know?"

There's a wealth within their happiness. Unfortunately, their plan is fundamentally flawed and most delusional. Q continues eating happily, clueless of the fact he's bedding down within striking distance of a most disturbed fiend.

The bastard Leroy. A bottled and condensed cruelty is stuck tight within Leroy. His veins run cold with something sadistic.

"And you?" Anna sputters. "Your story."

Sedative is her tone, and yet her query has me squirming. "My story?" I stammer. "There isn't much. I wed my husband at the age of seventeen." I pause. I've never heard my own story told aloud. It's spoken repeatedly within my own head like broken and wounded fragments of poetry, but I've never pieced it together in speech.

"We came here in hopes of becoming something more and became something…else."

Anna's grasp is fever-warm as she takes my hand. "Our stories…your story…is not finished. Much more to tell, you know?" Plush as cotton, the back of her cool hand is pressed to my cheek. "Much more to tell."

Am I more than what I am presently? Is there a future beyond this farm and the tears it's harvested from me? How might I save us? The three of us?

Dark comes the night; its fingers delve deep within my soul for a firm grasp. Leroy lies lifeless as I cower into the bedding and lie down with a devil.

My mind is a wind-whipped web of confusion and within that muddled mess is something resembling excitement. The mounting thought of running has my lips curling. The unknown…the vast greatness beyond this…just the idea germinates a sweltering exhilaration—something familiar.

Sleep evades me. Visions of a life elsewhere, petting a cat with a book in hand, have my eyelids electrified and incapable of sealing. The hours are seconds and any contentment is shattered with the shrieking of the alarm clock wailing through the darkness. It's early…too early.

He grumbles and mumbles and his moving mass disrupts my bedding. I hope the fields require his early departure. I pray my name evades his lips—

"Meyrick." My name bounces from the walls on his heavy breath.

"Yes, Leroy."

"Tug."

Repulsive as his demand is, he won't climb atop me, his swollen belly pressed to me—liquor-thick breath assailing my senses.

A timid spider, my hand crawls beneath the sheets to find his dank manhood, semi-aroused, as he sprawls and grunts. A chore…but then I do enjoy gathering eggs and even the wash is less than miserable. His breath…the tension within him as my hand moves about his thickening member, is nauseating. The sounds fill the room and enter my ears for several minutes.

His hideous moan, the uncomfortably firm grip on my hair and the warmth running over my grasp…he is finished with me and now he's pushing me away as if I'm the one who's unbathed and pungent.

"Clean that shit up! Eggs…bacon," he barks before stammering to the bathroom.

My hands and the morning are washed away. A

freshly washed face, and my attention is once again focused on the visiting duo.

Finding they're quarters without them has me perplexed. I hastily search about the farmyard to find they've vanished.

Welling tears spill to streak my face as I walk toward the woodlands. I take notice of nothing but the path before me. They're gone. They left so suddenly…*unless*…unless Leroy woke early to fetch them! The forest provides no answers to their whereabouts. The worn-trails I have grown to love are of no comfort now—I feel I am sinking into them. The ache of loneliness is more physical than that of any purpled bruise I've boasted. *Where are my strangers?*

Just before turning to return for the house, the sounds of something peculiar noose my attention. Laughter. I grin from my core upward.

Gathering the front of my gown, I race down the pathway toward the gleeful interaction. Off the path, through a clearing, I find my escape artists bathing happily in the pond. My smile broadens.

"Hello!" My call turns their faces to me.

They wave casually. So calm is the water on the opposing side of the pond that it resembles a mirror reflecting the tall trees encircling the semi-transparent waters the two are bathing in.

"Are…are you hungry?"

The pair begins moving slowly through the heavy water. Inch-by-inch it slides from their bodies, undressing them as I turn bashfully.

"So sorry!" Anna calls. "You. You join us."

Something wild within beckons me to tear free of my garments, laugh and run splashing into the water.

"Please. You join?" Her gentle prodding has my face turning from foliage and to the bathing pair. I'm initially taken aback by the beauty before me. They stare, wild-eyed and waist-deep, droplets diving and slinking from them.

An excitement has me spellbound. Guilt, or something resembling it, hangs just above me like a stretched cloud…unable to effectively rain down.

One step closer and my breath halts midway. The water cascades from Anna…or something else. She stands just meters before me, and I watch as tiny tributaries leave her dark hair, framing her face, and down blackened feathers on her chest, arms and torso—glimmering in the early-morning sun like glistening black rubies. The visual physically sets me off-kilter, as if I'm walking unaided on a whirling carousel. A second shaking glance reveals Q garbed in dripping feathers from his chest and arms as well.

"No!" I press my fingers to my closed eyes—driving them deep in an effort to obliterate the vision. Half-slouched, I hear the parting water as Anna and Q rush to my side.

"Are you okay?" Anna enquires.

There are no feathers. I look to see only flesh…only concerned expressions.

"I need to go. I must…I must go. I'll prepare breakfast."

I leave them dazed and dripping as I return home attempting to process what I've witnessed. Exhaustion…exhilaration…perhaps the combination of the two have manipulated my mind in a most menacing way.

Quivering near the stove in the kitchen, I attempt to

collect myself. An odd buzzing lingers just outside my ears like mechanical insects aching to invade.

"Calm yourself, Emily…breakfast—*oh!*" A pounding on the screen-door disrupts me from conversing with myself. The knocking continues until I make my way to greet the guest. Expecting to encounter the two careless stowaways, I'm taken aback to open the door to another party entirely. "Hel…hello, there," I mutter, my gaze piercing through the pepper-haired man who delivered Anna and Q to our farm.

His gray grin and weathered eyes are merely cloaking a demon within. This man is as sinister as a conniving wolf, stalking a calf, still wet and trembling.

"May I help you?"

He chuckles. His jeans are pressed, as is his pearl-snap shirt…as if he's planning to attend an auction or perhaps he has dinner plans. "I need to come in."

His English boasts only a mild accent…nothing like Anna's.

"Whatever for? Leroy isn't home."

His head cocks, his gaze sets. "Of course. He left early. Yes?"

The response has my mind racing with speculation, fragmented theories bouncing about my brain. "He did. Won't you…will you please…I'm not sure I understand."

He smiles once more…something softer. "Please. I need coffee. May I come in?"

Reluctantly, I stand aside and allow him passage. His thick boots clunk and echo through the kitchen as he walks past.

"I'll make coffee, but I need to know what it is…" *He wants them.* "No. You can't have them back."

His eyebrows, two black caterpillars, bow to each other as he scowls. "Pardon?"

"They're not yours. They're not your property and you can't just—"

"Ssshhh…woman. Quiet." He pats his thick, bronze belt buckle and grins once more.

An ache crawls upward within me. Helpless and useless, as if I'm suspended in a musty, decrepit web eternally with predatory beings drawing from me what they please. "The barn…in the barn."

My defeated tone and posture have him shaking his head and shrugging. "To the barn, beautiful."

Barefoot and poorly, the grass beneath me is plush and of some comfort as I lead this monster to Anna and Q's sanctuary. With every ounce of my being I hope they are still within the woods. My compromised psyche allowed this fiend to arrive in his chariot…that boisterous truck that echoes through the trees, much like Leroy's, but perhaps Anna and Q took notice and escaped deep within the surrounding woodlands.

"Here," I say, nodding toward the door.

"This is not what I was expecting. I'm only so lenient."

My hatred bubbles from my core and quivers my upper lip. I follow him through the door to see him scan the vacant area only briefly. Every inch of my skin twinges with a fury—fingernails burying into my palms. "Th…there." I point to Anna and Q's bed of hay.

"Whatever you say, beautiful."

To my surprise, he begins unbuckling his belt, his tight jeans sliding off like snakeskin with his back to me. He hums happily and tosses his clothing aside.

My confusion is overwhelming as he turns to me—entirely nude and massaging his nether region.

"What is this? I don't…I don't understand."

"Payment. Why aren't you undressed? Did Leroy not detail our agreement?"

Damn you, Leroy! Had I known this bastard was merely here for this, I would have been done with it by now—both body and sheets washed and him on his way—Anna and Q paid for with pleasures of the flesh.

"So, you're not here to take them?"

"Undress."

"Okay…please, turn around."

He smirks, chuckles, and then obliges.

She emerges as silent as the shadows that concealed her and moves over the barn floor as gracefully as the softest wind…pitchfork in her grasp. I feel as though I'm observing from another world, or even reading what I'm seeing rather than watching as four rusted prongs pierce through his midsection from behind and knock him to the ground. She continues pushing, her rage unleashed until she pins him to the earth beneath us.

"Anna!" I react.

Initially he remains still. Only the dust moves around us. His feet then thrash wildly, his hands move madly behind him to interpret this cruel confinement. His eyes are drenched in fear.

"You finish this, my beauty," she mutters before kissing my cheek with lips softer than feathers. She darts through the doorway and into the daylight, leaving me to find my senses.

I watch as he squirms beneath me—his screams are nauseating and steal my breath like calloused hands wrapping tightly around my windpipe.

"Help!"

My gaze bounces about the walls and settles on a hefty mallet. I retrieve it, only to stand above him a few moments more, gathering the strength to quell his cries.

Something ignites at my feet and moves upward. An odd excitement has my grasp tightening on the handle, my brow aching in anticipation, I inch closer—lip clenched within my bite. *Am I not more than an object? Am I not more than payment?* The world may not be mine, but I am not the world's…I am certainly not his.

I raise the mallet high above his head. Just as the darks of his defeated eyes meet my gaze, I deliver my judgment, final and solid. The action anoints my chest and face in a warm, crimson triumph.

I shakenly drop the mallet and fall backwards, vomiting on the ground next to me. Liberation has left me with a sour taste and yet, as I look at the lifeless fiend before me, I'm nearly inclined to wipe the retch from my mouth and grin. I am not his to take. He learned that today…I am not his.

3.

My feet pound the earth beneath me. Dappled in orange, yellow, and red, the trail leading from the community and into the woodland is well hidden under painted leaves. Any jagged things are concealed from my bare feet, too. Still, I run with all I have. Autumn air, uncomfortably brisk, pains my throat and dampens my eyes. I run until she is in my view...and then I am dismayed.

"Jennet! What!" I pause to digest what I'm witnessing. Jennet, my truest friend, my only friend, is wearing the typical ankle-length skirt—required of the girls and women of our community—but she's a bloodied mess. Her hands and the frontside of her garment are soaked in dark red.

"Are you hurt?" I wail out.

"No!" We rush to embrace one another and fall as one to our knees on the forest floor.

"Jennet, what is this? I'm petrified! What's happened?"

As we decouple, I witness any reserved strength leave her in fat, plentiful tears.

"Jennet tell me."

"Oh, Meyrick...I killed him," she whimpers. "I broke his skull with a rock."

There isn't one ounce of me remotely curious of who she is speaking of. A horrific feeling of implication engulfs me as she continues.

"Samuel came to me once more. I was gathering acorns. He...he wouldn't hear me. He wouldn't hear my words."

"What?"

"I told him no." Her voice quivers as she takes my hand—it's stained in a peeling and chipping burgundy.

"But Jennet, Samuel is your uncle. Did...did he—"

"Yes, Meyrick."

"And you, you did what?"

Her troubled gaze drifts past me as she points near a fallen tree. Slowly, I turn toward what could easily be mistaken for a sleeping gentleman with leaves scattered over him.

"Jennet," a sense of nausea has me swallowing hard, "Samuel is well regarded in the community. The Church will..."

"I know, Meyrick."

"Who...who else knows?" I blurt in a panic.

"Only you and Kaleb. He wouldn't leave my side until I demanded he fetch you."

"Was Kaleb here when Samuel attacked you? Can he validate the events?"

"No. He came upon us afterward, Meyrick. Kaleb's my brother. He wouldn't—"

"I'm not concerned with what he would or wouldn't do, Jennet. The cruel reality is, you are a girl and Samuel is a man of the Church. You know how this will end...it will end with reeds, and many of them—"

"No! No, Meyrick. Please." She clings to me, shaking as if her verdict has been read aloud. "Help me. Let us bury him or—"

"No. No, we won't. We will leave him where he lies, and we will never speak of this to anyone else. I'll fetch you clean clothes. We'll burn these, and this never happened...

***

The seconds have slipped away to form hours and

now the sun is painting the landscape on the western end of the hemisphere. The home is clean and prepared…as am I. The hammering in my chest reverberates throughout…the lovechild of exuberance and terror, it has me pacing, poised with eyelids peeled.

I've never longed for his return. To see him or hear him approaching has never brought me anything but anxiety. That changes today.

I steady my breath as the screen-door opens. His dingy gaze locks with mine. There's a hint of apprehension about his composure.

"How are you, dear?" Immediately I'm walking to him. My confident smile has his forehead creased.

"Meyrick?"

I chuckle. "Please. For the last time, Leroy. Meyrick is dead. *Dead*. My name is Emily."

Nostrils flair, eyes widen, his lips stiffen as if a word is stuck between them. He is dumbfounded.

"Shall we?" I motion to the door.

"What? What the hell has gotten into you, woman?"

Tilting my head, my grin is laced in sarcasm. "Nothing. Nothing at all."

"Where the fuck is Ricardo?"

"Oh. Was that his name? Please, follow me."

There's a palpable shift in the dynamics as he trails me down the drive to the smallest barn. The scents of the yard and fields have never been sweeter as I reach the splintered building.

Confidently, I open the door and motion him to walk past. No sooner does the ripe scent of soured-onion-body-odor assault my senses and he's belligerent.

"Damn you, Meyrick! I ain't got time for no bullshit, woman! What the hell is your crazy ass draggin' me out here for?"

My gaze bounces about the floor. There is no body, only a bed of hay and tiny dust particles swaying in and out of beams of light from above. "This makes no sense. He was…he was here."

"Ricardo?"

I turn to him. "The bastard you sent here to have his way with me! For payment!"

"Where is he, Meyrick? Did ya get him good n' paid?" Leroy chuckles.

My eyes could leap from my face like bullfrogs from the rage pulsating behind them. "I killed him, you bastard. I bashed his head."

Our stares remain stuck on one another's for several seconds until he smiles. "Liar. You ain't got it in ya."

My chest swells with pride as my gaze settles on the dark, damp bloody mess left where the body once was. "Oh! They…they must have…Anna and Q! Oh! My friends! Yes, my friends must have taken him away!"

I'm violently shoved aside as Leroy barrels past for a closer examination. "What is this, woman? What is this from?"

Standing proudly next to my work, I grin. "I told you. I killed him."

"No."

"Oh yes."

Reality sinks and settles as vigorous vulgarities leave his mouth in whispers. "Meyrick…what have you done? Do you know who this man was? Do you know what they'll do to me?"

If I could bottle his fear…capture it and lock it up tightly to ration and savor, how delightful that would be.

"Meyrick, this man was just one of many. More is gonna come. Why!" He turns to me. "Why would you do this!"

"To show you at long last that I am not your property to toss freely at your collectors as a means to pay debt."

"Stop! No more! This is real life! If you did this…if what you done is real…there's a heap a' hurt gonna come down on the both of us. A heap!"

His rage is convincing, and yet I'm not frightened by death.

"Let it come, Leroy. Be it the bottle or a blade, your end is near, regardless."

"Do you not hear what I'm saying to you, woman? If you really done did this, we're both as good as dead!"

"As good as dead? My dear, I've been worse than dead for ages. As good as dead sounds appealing. Indulge me the details."

His fear floods the dilapidated barn and encases us like a heavy syrup. His pacing slows as our gazes connect. "You, stupid bitch. Where the hell is he?"

"I don't know, Leroy. It appears my friends have disposed of him. I'm certain a variety of scavengers are picking about his remains as we speak."

"Friends? What friends is you talking about, you lunatic?"

My chuckle cuts through the atmosphere. "The people you brought here…promised better lives only to diminish their dreams. It seems we have developed a different agenda."

"I'm all but tired of your bullshit, woman. There ain't no makin' this right without some real thinkin' and plannin'. And yet…" His stare settles on the dirt floor, his brow creases as if he's processing intensely.

"This might just," he looks to me, "it might just work to our advantage."

His words are thorns—little barbs piercing my enthusiasm.

"With Ricardo gone, if he's really gone and they don't know you done what, this just might be a good thing, Meyrick."

His cheek twitches as if the brewing idea is conjuring a grin.

"Leroy."

I'm ignored. He mumbles and looks about the barn, plotting his conspiracy.

"Leroy!"

"What?"

"There are some mornings I walk the property and hear stirring from the cages you set around the barns. I'll find the rats you trapped with their mouths a bloody mess from chewing the cage wires. They pace and claw, desperate and anxious to flee back to the darkness. And do you know the difference between them and you?"

"What in the hell are you—"

"I'm there to free them mercifully so they can scamper away."

"Why on earth would you do such a thing?"

"Because almost all life has value. Almost all rats are worth saving…but not you." I turn for the door. "They will learn what happened here. Whoever these fiends are, the ones you speak of, they will find out what happened and when they do, I'll do nothing to protect you, even if it means my own end."

There's a distinguishable difference in temperature as I exit the barn. The air has never been calmer as I walk slowly toward the drive. If lit outside, a candle flame would have no breeze to dance on today and would be left to reach skyward. Too calm.

His grip on the back of my neck comes hard and heavy. So forceful is his grasp that I collapse into it.

"Leroy! Please!"

"Say it!"

Trees and other beautiful blooming things begin to blur in my tears. His breath, hot and pungent, comes hurling at me as pain sears and escalates.

"Now! Say it!"

"I'm…I am yours. I'm yours, Leroy." The relief is instant, and I'm tossed to the ground like a wet ragdoll. My face never touches the earth and my gaze settles on his tarnished boots.

"I'm takin' Ricardo's truck over the hill and past the crick bridge. I'll cut through the pasture to get home. You'd best have me a body by the time I get back, woman."

4.

"Jennet is jolly, Meyrick. Jolly Jennet. She's lucky for your friendship but you need to stop worrying so. It's nearly April. It's done with and we're okay. We're all going to be okay. You'll see."

"Stop talking, Kaleb. What's next?" I open my mouth like a child waiting for elixir.

"And this?" The metallic underbelly of a spoon rests on my tongue as the sweetest substance spills over. I sigh, sucking the utensil before he pulls it away.

"Easy. Honey," I reply.

"You can't do that." His words trace my cheek and ignite my senses.

"Do what?" I ask as my face flushes.

"You can't call me honey until we're married. It's the rules."

Like the substance in my mouth, I'm liquifying and on the verge of slipping down into an abyss. "You silly boy. Take the blindfold off me."

Girls with shy smiles and boys with blue eyes—the mundane is all around us and yet we'll never be in its center when we're together. His eyes are greener than the fields in spring and my grin is anything but bashful.

"Your turn." I stand from the wooden chair in my parents' kitchen and motion him to sit as I slide the blindfold from his grasp.

"My turn?" His grin fills my core with something more vibrant than butterflies...something more aggressive.

"Sit down. I'll have to learn your favorite things if I'm to cook for you once we're...if we are to be married."

He smirks while taking his seat. I gently maneuver the blindfold over his dark brown hair.

"I can cook for myself, Meyrick. I can cook for the both of us. You'll be busy writing and exploring."

"You can cook?" I reach for a jalapeno.

"I can do anything I set my mind to and so can you. If we believe in that we're going to be okay." He reaches forward blindly and smiles contently the instant I take his hand. "I love you, Meyrick."

I replace the Jalapeno with a salted slice of tomato. "And I love you."

"Hello?"

Nostalgia shattered, I look from my hands, trembling and folded atop the kitchen table, and to the front door. "Oh! You're back! Anna!"

"This is okay? This is okay that we're here?" She waits politely at the door until I usher the two of them inside.

"Of course. Where else are you supposed to be?"

After seating them at the table I make my way to the refrigerator. "What would you like to eat?"

The kitchen is soon thick with the smell of porkchops and rolls.

"I'd like to thank the both of you for doing what you did, but as soon as we're done here, I need you to take me to him."

Anna peers up from the plate I set in front of her. "Why?"

"I need to know where you took that man's body. More people are coming here and if they find him, they might hurt me."

"*Him.* They'll hurt him."

I kneel to her. "I assume that's true as well."

"No one would believe you would do such ugly things…but he is a monster, yes?"

"Yes, he is. Eat, and then you will take me to the body and we can discuss what we need to do."

"Nothing. There is nothing to do but wait."

"You're right. The logical thing to do is wait. I can't shake the feeling that I'm being still when I shouldn't be."

"What is there to do, Emily? Let them come…if they are coming, then they will come whether you are still or not."

"You're right. And when they do, we'll toss him to the wolves like the scraps he is," I exclaim.

"Si, but Emily, those wolves are dangerous. Remember how you came to be."

The sentence hits hard enough to knock the breath from me and leaves me unable to immediately respond.

"What do you know?" I finally sputter.

"I know your story is not done. So much left to tell, my beautiful. No more worrying. You know this story…how it ends, yes?"

"Ends? No. I'm afraid I have no crystal ball."

"Emily. So beautiful and strong." Pale light shimmers scantily in her eyes. She arrived in rags, tattered, torn and penniless, and yet if the sky fell like stone-shattered glass she'd be likely to survive. She's cold, cunning, and resourceful. She's dangerous, but there's a beauty in her danger.

Q. Baby-faced and typically noiseless—I wonder if he's as naïve as I assume. I turn my attention to him.

"*Oh!*" My gaze lands on my reflection in the blinking black avian eye of an abnormally large raven perched upon the chair top where Q had been seated.

"No! This…this cannot be!" Eyes sealed, I turn blindly in the opposing direction.

"Emily!" Anna calls after me as her chair scoots and crashes to the floor.

Eyes now pried, a quick glance about the area reveals no winged things. There are only two sets of anxious eyes…beautiful brown eyes coursing with concern.

"Emily?"

"I'm…excuse me." The screen-door is teeming with marauding insects, all craving the light within. I exit the home and make my way down the cement steps and into the darkest parts of the night. The parts with little room for starlight or pale beams escaping the windows behind me.

"Emily, wait!" Her calls cascade to cover me like fresh sheets atop a stained and ugly mattress. I have no choice but to turn to her as she runs to me.

"Anna…I…"

"You are angry with us?"

"You? No. No, not in the slightest." Palm pressed to my forehead, I look from her and to the dark.

"Emily—"

"I need the night! I need the dark! My eyes see what isn't…my head…my mind isn't right."

As tears fall there's no hesitation in her embrace. It's genuine and full.

"Oh, Anna, why are you so kind to me? You have nothing. At any moment the very breath you draw could be stolen and yet you comfort me. Why?"

"Emily, you have seen this story, yes? Our story…you know how it ends, this beautiful tragedy."

Her words are blacker than any corner of night I

seek, yet they lack logic and have me pulling from her—staring her in the eyes.

"Emily—"

"Anna, I must go. My head isn't right."

Her firm grasp tugs me as I turn to leave. "Your heart, Emily."

"What?"

"Is your heart right? If so, we can fix the rest. Promise." She clutches my finger.

"Come from the dark. If there are beautiful things there, you cannot see them. If there are ugly things there, you cannot see them seeing you. Come, back to the light, my beautiful."

I trail her, this vagrant, gypsy-like beauty with a hypnotic ability to calm my raging seas. And yet, even as she guides me hand-in-hand, my gaze hesitantly settles on the absurdity just before me. From behind, her head is unmistakably draped in a shimmering onyx of fine feathers. My squinting eyes beg to look from what they're witnessing, and yet the vividness of what is before me as she leads has my sight transfixed. The approaching light dances in the pristine plumage—so exquisitely detailed it can't be an illusion. Somewhat terrified, mostly mesmerized…I trail her at an arm's length and just as we approach the home the feathers are blinked away.

"Emily." Anna turns to me; her gorgeous dark hair is nothing more than hair. There's nothing avian-like about her.

"Y…yes?"

"I promise. We can fix it."

5.

Like dough from the countertop, my face peels from the kitchen table. It's morning. I must have drifted to sleep last night once my mind had toppled completely. Natural light works its way around the kitchen curtains to penetrate the stagnant atmosphere. It's cool, calm, and uncharacteristically silent for daybreak. I spring from the chair to investigate.

"Anna? Q?" Tearing through the home reveals no signs of life.

I race to their barn, calling out their names. A dramatic entrance reveals nothing in here either.

My head is sick with what feels like all the bad parts of wine…as if all the poisons of the worst merlot have been filtered and condensed and prepared in a glass for me to consume ten times over. Processing is slow and ineffective like my mind is congested—a pneumonia of the brain.

"Meyrick." His cold voice is just behind me in the doorway.

"Yes…Leroy."

"This, *Anna and Q*, I hear you screeching for, who and where are they?"

"The people you summoned. The farmhands Ricardo came to collect payment for. I don't know where they—" My head snaps backwards on a floppy neck as I'm violently shoved or kicked to the ground from behind. I meet the floor with impressive and blackening force. The air has completely escaped my body, and when I regain it in a full, deep, and choppy breath, I take in with it all the filth stirred from the dusty, dirt floor.

He laughs as I cough and choke and roll to my side. "That's right, nasty barn whore. You stay down there where you belong."

"Pl...please."

He moves closer like a vulture hopping alongside a dying deer. "I didn't know I had farmhands here, woman. My debt to Ricardo had nothin' to do with no farmhands. Hell, if I could get me some hands just by tossin' some pink at a motherfucker, I'd be right as rain." He spits at the ground beside me. "Why was this kept from me?" he asks, squatting to me.

"Please, Leroy—"

"Answer me!"

"I told you—"

"You went on about some crazy bullshit, but I didn't know I had hands headed this way! Where are my hands, Meyrick!"

My tears dot the dirt beneath me. "I need them."

"What?"

"I need them, Leroy."

His expression softens. His fists unclench. "You really are a fuckin' loon, Meyrick. Get up."

His shoulders nearly touch either side of the doorframe as he leaves me pathetically splayed out on the dirt-floor.

I close my eyes as I cradle my head into the bend of my arm. My mind swirls and sways as if I'm sailing through the air on a swing-set with my eyes sealed. The dirt is inches from my face...inches...

"Where's your face, Meyrick?"

"My lord and family I have hurt...and so I'm cast onto the dirt," I sob.

Belly down in the dirt, my entire face is in agony,

but my nose especially aches for reprieve. A blurry brown soil is just before me. Within my peripheral view are ankle-length skirts and trousers resting on dusty boots. They've gathered round to bear witness to my punishment. Each breath I draw is rich in an organic musk and brings with it bits of debris.

"And what do you ask of your people, Meyrick? What is your penitence?"

My mind's a muddled mess. The words are there—heavy like a fog, yet I can't grasp them.

"Meyrick!"

"By...by the trail...or, or by the reed? Do I walk? Or...or do I bleed?"

The words are a vile venom seeping from me. Countless times I've pitied those in this position, face to the earth like carrion and awaiting the mob's macabre verdict. Walking the outskirts for seven days and seven nights continuously, stopping only when they collapse from exhaustion...or be lashed by designated members of the Community with thin, sturdy reeds along the back, buttocks, and legs until the ground beneath them is quenched in crimson.

Either option is barbaric, but the latter has sent grown men to an early grave.

"Father—"

"Silence, Meyrick!"

His boot, the same boot I've polished lovingly hundreds of times, comes into view. I wonder if he's breaking inside. I wonder, while he stares down on me from above, if he's crumbling...even fractured mildly. I'm completely fragmented as I hear the first response.

"Walk," says the trembling voice of Jennet. I pray her courageous leap will set off a cascade of identical

replies.

"Let me remind you all," my father addresses them, "the girl you see disgraced beneath you was witnessed leaving my home with a man she refuses to identify!" He isn't fractured. He's solid stone.

His hastening pace kicks rubble into my face. "What deeds took place under my roof? What deeds took place under your watch?"

"Reed." Another man's voice says. Followed by another.

"No. Walk!"

The crowd around me is erupting in dispute until at last my father's voice cuts through the chaos to quiet them. "As a Church Leader and Community Justice, it is my duty to deliver a verdict when one cannot be reached. However, being this…woman's father, clouds my ability to do God's work today. Bartholomew, as a senior Church advisor, the decision is yours."

My pulse races. My breath is nearly uncatchable as the group around me goes silent.

"I've known this girl her entire life." I hear Bartholomew's weathered voice proclaim. "Call me naïve, but you have yet to convince me she's been down to the Devil's business."

I nearly cry out.

"It is always a poor decision for a girl to entertain a man in solitude prior to a holy union. And for that reason, I pray this girl has a decent pair of boots. She's got a deal of walking to do."

***

The sun's rays remain bashfully tucked beyond the tallest of the trees, as if they're afraid to kiss my face. I move slowly from the barn. There's something pitiful in walking back to what breaks me but historically I've made such walks often.

I've never strolled upstairs or through a front door of a home that I regarded as wholesome or welcoming. A pervasive sense of unrest has engulfed every dwelling I've resided. I read of characters rushing through the front doors of their homes and feeling at peace. It seems humans are always trying to go home or reminisce on happier days. Perhaps we're trying to get back "there," or back to our fondest stretch in life. What if that stretch doesn't exist? What if our happiest times are mere fragments scattered over years of scars?

Once inside I quickly disrobe and fetch fresh attire while listening to Leroy urinate and hum in the adjoining bathroom.

In the kitchen I take to my chores mindlessly as if I'm not guilty of murder and absent my accomplices. Leroy too appears less impacted as his hands intrusively prod and feel me from behind while I stand at the sink.

Knowing any second his demand, revolting and stanch, will spill from his mouth, I opt instead to dry my hands and preemptively walk toward the bedroom.

As I turn I glance at what must be an illusion. A slender black feather is resting on the floor near the kitchen table. It stares at me, taunting me. It's an odd thing, to feel one's sanity slipping away like fine sand and be helpless to stop it.

"You headin' somewhere?" he asks before reaching down the front of his jean shorts to scratch himself.

"The bedroom, Leroy." Subtle and monotone, my stare stays firm on the feather.

"Don't let me stop ya, woman."

I only nod.

"What the hell are you lookin—"

"Something that isn't there, Leroy! Why do you care?"

Without looking at him I can feel his expression. He's flabbergasted, irritated, and every line on his face will be especially pronounced.

"What the fuck does that mean, Meyrick?"

I look to him to find he's exactly as I pictured. "My mind isn't right."

"Ya don't say."

"It's all…it's all I have left and it's leaving me." My cracking voice seems to elicit his amusement. A crooked grin creeps across his engorged face.

"What you done was nuts, Meyrick. I mean nuts—"

"I'm talking about something else entirely." I shake my head. "Look there, by the table leg. What do you see?"

"Huh?"

"What do you—"

"Goddamn, woman. I see a clothespin and a bird feather."

"What?" I shout, studying his face.

"I said, I see—"

"You can see that black feather?" I exclaim.

Like a swollen swine, he grunts and groans, places his hands on his knees and bends over for a closer inspection. To my amusement, he retrieves the feather from the floor and presents it to me. Clasped between his leathery thumb and index, the black feather is nothing worth a second glance, but in this moment it's the most beautiful thing on earth.

"It's real. You can hold it." A tear etches its way to

the floor as I take the feather from him.

"What in God's name? Meyrick, we gotta whole coop fulla' feathers. If that's all it takes ta keep you happy, you know where that shit's at, you nut."

"I don't have time to explain. I need to find them."

"The fuckin' feathers?"

"No…"

"I see. Your refugees?" There's a shift in his tone; it's darker. Any light in his eyes empties like milk from the bottom of a broken jar.

"I need to find them, Leroy." He grabs my forearm as I attempt to maneuver around him.

"Yes, you do, little lady. You fetch them hands and bring them on back so we can have a discussion about farm livin'. I'll put a hurt on them like they ain't never felt until they choke out the location of that body."

My arm is freed in one forceful pull. Outside once more, I make my way to the thicket.

I'm disheartened to find they're not near the pond. Perhaps the entirety of the situation proved too much. Perhaps they're blazing through the woods in search of something more than hay for bedding and a watchkeeping devil.

A fallen tree beckons me to be seated and so I oblige. Off the trail the trees appear adjoined by dense vines. The woodland is the perfect place to hide or to become lost. The idea of being left behind to rot like the log I'm sitting on has me decomposing inside already.

The feather I hold further perplexes me. Submitting to the idea of insanity was simpler. A painful past riddled with awful secrets such as mine could have anyone's psychology challenged. Now this object, its physicality, challenges that and leaves me with questions for which there are no earthly answers.

With so many circumstances, the simplest solution is to look away…to push it to the back or the brink and pretend it doesn't exist. That option isn't here now.

Perhaps they have fled, perhaps they're traipsing about the area just waiting for an opportunity to return. Regardless, I have no alternative but to refocus.

A vehicle's engine echoes throughout the trees. We have visitors.

From the tree-line, yet well tucked and concealed, I spy Leroy happily engaged in conversation with a heavyset Latino gentleman at the base of the porch. Their words are swallowed up in the blue truck engine's roar prior to entering my ears.

The encounter appears cordial yet even from the thicket Leroy's apprehension is painted blatantly in apparent expressions and stiffened movements. If there wasn't cause for suspicion prior to this encounter, I'm confident there is now.

A sunset colored in the richest reds and yellows couldn't rival the beauty of intimidation stamped on Leroy's face. The wide-eyed, lip-licking fool appears as though he's before God Almighty, confessing his darkest deeds.

A few more moments of this interaction and I watch the gentleman return to his vehicle and drive away.

Like a weary barn cat, I approach the home in an uneasy way. I find Leroy in the living room, arms crossed and in a trance.

"Leroy?"

Much to my astonishment, he turns to me boasting a wolfish grin. "I think we done did it, Meyrick!"

I step backwards. "Oh?"

"Antonio just said they found't Ricardo's truck up a country mile. The whole lot of 'em don't know what to think about it. Every idea from tequila and hookers to he done got snatched up by the Alvidrez boys." He moves closer. "I just hope ain't no doubt on us—on this farm. I pray I convinced that boy—"

"You were marvelous, Leroy," I state confidently as I unfold my arms and force a smile.

"Come again."

"I witnessed the encounter from the bushes. There wasn't the slightest hint of guilt about your expression. If anything, you appeared concerned and genuine."

My words swell his chest and widen his smile. "Well, if you say so, little lady."

"I do, Leroy. I most certainly do."

"We need that body, Meyrick." His eyes and tone attempt to connect as if we're abettors to some ill-planned conspiracy. It's revolting.

"I understand, Leroy. I'll find the farmhands—"

"You don't need whoever the fuck you been galivanting around with, Meyrick. Strap-on some lady-boots and do some real searchin'. This here is all but pulled off if we can get our hands on that maggot meat."

I nod obligingly and turn to leave.

6.

"If I ever leave here, I want away from all of it. I want it all to melt away just like this."

We stand under budding branches. The sound of muck is all around us and our boots squelch in puddles beneath us. What is left of winter is retreating from the treetops in heaps of dirty-white, crashing to the muddy forest floor.

"But look what it uncovers once it's melted, Meyrick," Jennet stammers.

The diminished remains of Samuel lie at our feet. He's been preserved well enough under a blanket of winter, but evidence of nibbling scavengers is prevalent on Samuel's blackened fingers and face.

"They think he's left," Kaleb interjects. "The Church thinks he's abandoned the Community. Even our father believes it to be true."

"He never left," Jennet snaps. Her tone is colder than the wind wafting through the trees. "He's always been here, just waiting to expose me for who I am."

"And who are you, precisely?" I ask.

"I'm Jennet, the murderess. I'm destined to face the reeds, and if they don't put me in the ground, I'll eventually go there an unlovable, scarred, childless hag!" she proclaims angrily at the body beneath us.

"Enough. That isn't true."

"Isn't it, Meyrick?" she hisses.

"You are Jennet McCormick," I say kindly. "You are kind. You are gentle. And you are guilty of nothing. Nothing here would have the Church casting their suspicion on you."

She exhales completely while nodding, as if my

words have penetrated to make sense. "I too want it all to melt away. I want the snow to take him with it."

"The snow won't, my friend. The Summer heat and rain will. You'll see. He won't be long for this world. And I assure you, your actions are forgiven in the next."

We walk wobbly as fresh fawns through the slick surroundings leading back to the Community. The extent of our struggles—hands extended for balance, Kaleb falling to the mud, seems to elicit a few chuckles as if we're not once again leaving a monster to decay into nothingness.

"Meyrick," Jennet says softly as the trees thin and the outskirts come closer into view.

"Yes?"

"Before he's taken by the heat and rain...just before, I'd like to return. I'd like to witness him at his foulest and know it's due me. Do you find that odd?"

"Attagirl!" his voice rattles me. "Your friends didn't drag the bastard far, did they?"

Behind the small barn, surrounded by tall weeds and grimy farm equipment lies the body of Ricardo, face-up, with an open mouth. Dirt and debris cling to his sunken, cyanotic eyeballs. There's little to no color variation in his face and exposed gums and swollen tongue.

"You startled me, Leroy." I watch him slide between the barbed wire fence as limberly as a fourteen-year-old schoolboy.

"Startled ya?" he echoes. "Oh, Meyrick. You're a cold-blooded killer now. If you go round gettin' spooked every time a good ol' boy like myself says hello you'll be the shortest lived killer in history."

Traipsing through the weeds, he makes his way to stand at my side. Gleaming eyes give the impression he's admiring the work before us as if it's a rare painting rather than a bloating body.

"I wasn't anticipating building a repute, Leroy." I chuckle.

"A what?"

The totality of the situation leaves me with a different sense of sickness bubbling in my belly. It isn't the myriad, minuscule beetles crawling clumsily about my victim's face, hair, and unguarded eyes. It isn't the soft hint of death's scent carried on an early morning breeze or the fresh memory of my quarry's cries beneath me. The nauseating camaraderie fermenting here, side by side with him, has me longing for a glimpse of what the end might look like. I might dance with a devil if it sits me front row to his execution.

"I simply meant, I don't think I'll go about killing anyone else. What's next, Leroy?"

"Where's my hands, woman?"

"I don't know, Leroy. I promise I do not know…perhaps they fled."

He looks to the sky, apparently pondering. "Well, we'll just have to keep the lookout for 'em, won't we?"

"Indeed."

As if he's congratulating me on a prized bull, he pats my back with an unsavory gentleness that is most uncharacteristic. "Now I'ma dig a hog roastin' pit. Why don't you go fix us up a celebratory breakfast…anything smothered in maple syrup would please me at the moment."

I offer a courteous smile before collecting the front of my gown and stepping over ivy and carnage to make my way from the mayhem.

"Meyrick," he calls to me."

"Yes…Leroy?"

"You done good."

In the kitchen I apply a generous application of mentholated jelly inside my nostrils to mask the residual odor.

An iceberg of Crisco slowly vanishes into an oily ocean within a warming skillet. There's nothing pleasing in preparing meals for monsters. *Am I a monster?*

I crack a large, white egg and empty it into the oil. It crackles and gurgles and pops. So overpowering is the lingering scent of my crime that even the smell of sizzling bacon is imperceptible. Like a wasp, his death seems to have grown angry and followed me into the home.

The second egg cracks against the countertop within my grasp. Just above the heated skillet I watch its solid contents fall flailing from a blue eggshell to the hot oil. To my horror, a tiny, pink bird now thrashes before me, cooking alive.

"Oh!" Both hands on the handle, I toss the skillet and all its contents to the kitchen sink and immediately begin to run cool water. "Oh, no, no, no! A raven's egg?"

Obstructed by a dishtowel, the water rises in the sink to create an oily mess as I bring myself to turn it off. When I remove the skillet, I'm taken aback to find nothing but partially cooked chicken eggs, two of them. Near my foot I spot the shell I tossed just moments prior. It isn't blue in the slightest. It's as white as the first. The sink and stove are searched for good measure but within seconds I'm cursing myself and reheating the skillet. Perhaps I'd allot the appropriate amount of concern to the matter if I hadn't just been with the body of the man I murdered. And yet, this is no feather I can hold within my grasp to prove its presence. This is some contortion of reality that I cannot begin to understand. *To the back or to the brink.* Such trickery of the mind cannot be explained away while dappled in cooking oil and streaked in yolk. Explaining to Leroy why breakfast has yet to be prepared is another matter I wish to avoid. Hesitantly, I retrieve two additional eggs…both white.

An hour passes before Leroy barrels through the screen-door—dirt avalanches off his trousers and boots and trails him to the kitchen table where he plops in a most dramatic fashion.

"I can't fuckin' believe them folks at Sam's Funeral charge the heap they do for tossin' a meat sack in the ground and sprinklin' dirt on top." One after the other, his boots are kicked from his feet to thump to the floor.

"Thank you for doing that, Leroy. Here's your breakfast."

Even as the plate is set before him I'm examining the fried eggs for any signs of life. A sticky sponge, his tongue drags across his chapped, peeling lips, and his eyes gleam with anticipation like hasn't eaten in days.

"This looks damn good, Meyrick. Damn good. Smothered, just like I asked for."

"I hope you enjoy it." Hands clasped before me, I stand tableside as he cuts through eggs, bacon, and soaking hotcakes and tosses and smears the contents all about until his plate resembles a repulsive pile of vomit.

"You bet your sweet little biscuits I will." The first

dripping heap is shoveled in. "Ain't no one gonna find that bastard." The words come through as he chews.

"Oh?" I pull a chair from the table.

"Get me some coffee before you sit down," he snarls. "He's not only in the ground, he's under a mess of barnwood, weeds and a tractor tire thata' liked to thrown out my goddamned back!"

"Here's your coffee, Leroy. Tell me, why was that man so important? Who was he?"

Another oozing fork-full is shoved in. A greasy, yellow stream tears down his stubbly chin. "He was a problem, woman. One what we done solved. As the woman of the house…all you need to know is it was tended to and he's in the ground."

I nod. "I understand."

"But that don't mean you didn't do your part, Meyrick. Don't go to thinkin' I'm tickled pink you done run off and kill't a man for trying to collect on what was rightfully his. But what you done is gonna make things a heap easier round here now that that bastard is in the grave."

Each inch of my skin sears in fury staring down on him. His words pummel firmer than a father's fist. *I might dance with a devil…* And so, I exhale.

"Leroy, on the subject of graves," I take my seat, "when might you take me?"

He pulverizes what is in his mouth while leaning back. "Where? Take you where…Meyrick?"

"I only want pay my respects. I need closure—"

"You can pay that respect from here. *Don't ask me that shit again!*" Flared nostrils and widened eyes remind me of the temper prowling just beneath the skin—reminds me this sloppy mess of man gains agility and predatory reflexes with the slightest provocation.

Again I nod, several times, as I slide my hand across the table to rest atop his. "I'm…I'm sorry. Please."

He says nothing but takes up his fork once more. The gesture assures I won't be left broken and bleeding, face to the hardwood, wondering if this day is my last— split lip curling in a simper at the idea of finality. "I'll warm your coffee, Leroy."

7.

Walls hold history like jars do fireflies. They seem safe enough in their structure, but the world is free to cast a curious glance.

The walls of the Community Library house some of my happiest history. The hours spent here are never wasted. I could consume shelves of books of every genre and be left ravenous for more. Each page…word, brings with it escape to another world.

I've never left the Community, other than wandering about the forest trails. We're insulated among the trees and hills, tucked in at dusk within our modest, mossy homes. 'Yesterday's ways are the ways of the Lord.' Yet, according to the books I read, there isn't much about the ways of the Community that parallel any outside traditions—new or old. Cruelty is a common element, it seems, in any equation involving humanity, but I'd stretch to say a book highlighting my life and how I came to be, might be considered peculiar if it were stumbled upon outside the Community.

Two tables away, my father sits stoically with a pipe in one hand and a worn book in the other. The air is thick with the scents of fine tobacco and aged literature. The Church and the Library are more than places to worship and read. The buildings act as dual pinnacles within the Community. In and around either building, the Community mourns, educates, casts judgment, celebrates, and seeks shelter.

A slender collection of poetry lies open before me— Emily Dickinson. Her words leave me lost in contemplation. Such power in a pen—each emotion is impacted.

The words still warm, I turn to page one to relish its splendor yet again.

"You do love that, don't you?" Kaleb whispers as he sits across the table from me.

"Quiet, Kaleb. My father is just there."

"Why?" He leans forward, grinning.

"Why what? I don't want to be disruptive—"

"Why Emily Dickinson?"

I'm nearly appalled by the question. "She's brilliant...she's...she's innovative and inspiring and was all of those things at a time when she wasn't supposed to be."

He smirks. "You'd make a fine Emily."

Instant redemption. "Well, I'm flattered. Now please, I don't want to draw attention."

"Meyrick, may I speak with your father tonight?" His eyes gleam in the dimly lit room.

"I suppose you may speak to him anytime you please." My attempt to remain expressionless is useless as I hide my smile under my hand.

"Will you be my bride, Meyrick?"

"You can't ask me that, you daft boy. You must get permission from my father. And I've walked, Kaleb. Do you want a shamed bride?"

He only smiles. His hand slides over the oak table to take mine—I instantly recoil. "Kaleb. You're being reckless."

"Be my bride."

"I will not. Not until you honor my father by seeking his permission."

"He has, my dear." My father's voice resonates from just behind me.

"What?" I look to either of them, dumbfounded.

"You, co-conspirators! This was planned?"
Kaleb nods while standing. "So?" He shrugs.
"Of course!"

A truck door slams closed and my eyes open. There are no fine books here, only a few almanacs and the filthy magazines Leroy finds pleasure in. The sheets and bedding are in disarray. I wake to daylight cloaked in gray. The kind of daylight that leaves one puzzled on awakening as to whether it is morning or evening.

Wits regained, I realize I'm waking from an afternoon nap. What I'm unsure of, however, is who is knocking on the front door.

A glance in the bathroom mirror and I'm making my way toward the hammering reverberating throughout the home. I open the door to the same gentleman who'd visited just this morning.

"May I help you?" I ask.

"No. No, ma'am. Is Señor Leroy home?" he asks softly.

I open the screen-door. "I'm unsure where he is. May I interest you in some tea or coffee? I'm sure he'll be home soon."

With his eyes closed, he politely shakes his head no. "Ma'am, it's important that I speak to Leroy. Very important. You don't know where I could find him?" His stare locks with mine.

"I don't. He left while I was napping."

"Too bad," he replies before turning to waddle down the crumbling cement porch steps.

"And what was your name, sir?"

"Antonio," he replies over his shoulder.

"I'm Emily. It's nice to have met you." I walk casually from the home, allowing the screen-door to slam behind me. "Antonio, you might check the barns. He could be out tinkering with equipment, or whatever you boys do in barns." I chuckle as I descend.

"Oh, I don't see his truck here, ma'am," he replies courteously.

"No, but he's been spending a great deal of time out there just the same, mainly in the smallest of the three. It wouldn't kill you to look."

His smile fades. No words are spoken. He nods politely before walking past me and down the dirt drive to pay homage at the shallow grave of a monster.

8.

Evening tea and a whippoorwill's call—both are typically comforting. Anxiety has me sipping with shaking hands and taking for granted the night's orchestra while seated on the porch. The tea's attempt to calm my buzzing brain is futile.

Leroy is late from the fields and his absence leaves me wondering if my disclosure led to something colorful. Thoughts of him arriving bruised and bleeding, tearing through the doorway and seeking retribution, have my teacup trembling within my grasp.

I imagine Anna and Q and where they might be. I'm hopeful they've found safe and suitable lodgings. The area is speckled with modest farms operated by cheap labor and overzealous ambitions.

A soft rumble of thunder in the distance hints at a possible rain. The air slithering around me is cool and freshly scented. Rejuvenation. The tree tops dance in the dying auburn glow to a rustling symphony. Like lanky scarecrows animated by sorcery, they bob and sway eerily as if provoking the sky to pour. I now walk among them on the trails. If the wind could only take my sorrows and fling them away…

I cast my gaze skyward. Willow sprays frame the twilit sky like locks of harlot hair. All around me things float on the breeze…swirling through the branches and caressing my skin.

"F…feathers?" I freeze. Black feathers float on the gusts encircling me as if they're atop a stream bound for a pond. "This cannot be." I squeeze my eyes closed. Like a mad woman I claw the air collecting the free-floating feathers as they fly by. Fists full, I tear from the trees and toward the house—toward Leroy's truck. He is home.

Up the stairs and through the door, I'm nearly relieved to find Leroy whistling and preparing a beverage at the kitchen.

"Leroy!" My exhilarated entry startles him.

"What?" His drink topples into the sink.

"Leroy, the woodland! It's cursed! There's an evil there!" My screeching is coupled with handfuls of feathers held just in front of his bewildered face.

"What in God's name are you talkin' about, you fuckin' lunatic?"

"The feathers! These black feathers!" I shake my hands violently until he grabs either of the them.

For several seconds he stares at my fists before turning to the sink once more. "Meyrick, when a horse or a…mule goes nutty, a farmer does right by that beast and puts a barrel to its head. I could do right by you," he turns to me, "but then what would this *rat* have to stick his dick in?"

Glass in hand, he walks past me as I look to my trembling hands—each of them clenching a few brown leaves. "No. How can that be?"

"You're nutty as fuck is how," he replies from bedroom.

"I need help, Leroy. Please."

He responds with a low chuckle.

"Leroy." I enter the room. "My mind is behaving bizarrely."

"Well, you've got bigger problems. What'd your crazy-ass tell that ol' boy today?" he snarls.

"What?"

The drink he prepared is gulped down in three

swallows. "Antonio."

Silence and alcoholic odors fill the room before I shrug. "I told him you would be home soon. He was persistent and insisted on looking about the property."

Staring at the floor as he walks to me nodding, he replies in a low tone, "I can dig as many holes as I gotta. You just keep 'em comin'."

He leaves me with a chill that could rival a Canadian December.

My mind is as disheveled as the bed I sit upon. As the rain begins pelting the roof and windows, I rest my head to the pillow. The world fades into the backs of my eyelids. The day is done.

"Have you given thanks today, Meyrick?" His question comes slow, like cold honey.

"Several times, Father. There is much to be thankful for."

"Indeed."

I feel his gaze on me as I bring the quilt to my chin. "Goodnight, Father."

He emerges from the hallway's shadows to stand in the doorway of my bedroom. "Meyrick."

"Yes, Father."

"When he takes your hand tomorrow and you are unified before your community and your lord, know that you are unworthy of the hand you are taking. Know that Kaleb's love blinds him, and that blindness is to your benefit. Know that if you forgo the daily regimen of pleading for forgiveness, your sacred union will wilt and die by the hand of the Lord."

He moves closer—his footsteps are angry. "Do you not hear me?"

"I do, Father."

"Kaleb is a good man. He deserves more than a tarnished bride."

"Tarnished?" I arise in bed. "Father, I'm not."

"You deserved the reeds, Meyrick!" I've never heard my father yell so loud.

"I walked, Father. I walked all seven—"

"You should be walking still, you harlot! You whore! You are your mother. You're one and the same! I can only pray Kaleb is a stronger man than I, and he can tame what brews within you!"

Tears streak my cheeks. I'm left speechless until I hear his belt buckle unfastening. "Father, please. If I'm bruised tomorrow...on my wedding day."

He tears the belt from his waist and yanks the quilt from atop me. "You are under my roof and my rule for this night. You will obey me as the man of the house, even if it breaks you!"

I merely nod and stand to remove my nightgown for the lashing. When my garment falls from my head to the floor, he is gone—walking back to the shadows with belt in hand.

A thunderous crack yanks me from slumber and my childhood home. The hanging fixtures flicker and quiver under the violent downpour. The windows are framed rivers on the walls.

I find Leroy in the kitchen, his face plastered to the table and pooled in copious drool. If nature's rage won't rile him, I won't attempt either. I collect a quilt and retire to the sitting room. So deafening are the sounds of the storm in this area of the home that my voice is silenced as I gently call out from the divan, "Hope is the thing with feathers."

The noise drives from every angle, leaving me

riddled with a suffocating anxiety I can only liken to having a pillowcase secured over my face as a child by juvenile playmates. It leaves little room for thinking, and yet, given my undeniably compromised physical and emotional state, perhaps that is best.

Reality…illusion…the inability to distinguish between, and yet I remain cognizant of the issue. And now, as I look through this wet window, this framed river, are these lights bobbing through the dark genuine?

Pouncing from the divan to the window frame, I glare through the downpour. Blurred lights, possibly lanterns, are fading into the night as they move closer to the barns.

Are these welcome intruders or has my mind created yet another vivid fiction?

The lights sink into dark. If there are unannounced guests roaming the property, I'm certain they know just what they're looking for and perhaps where to begin their search. Only time will tell.

I retreat to the divan and under my quilt. Thoughts of what tomorrow might bring aren't easily seized as the rain remains entirely oppressive. I once again close my eyes…and fade.

9.

"The union of marriage is one of beauty. It is one of endurance."

Kaleb's parents, my father, and Jennet are all that are present to witness the unification. Only a handful of disgraced brides have been successfully wed to other members from our community. The majority live quiet, solitary lives or leave...consumed by the trees, never to be seen again.

I feel my father's eyes on me like November-chilled air through a wind-shook door. The preacher's words can't come fast enough. Such simple phrases, yet they relinquish so much.

"For decades our ways have puzzled those who pry and prod," the preacher continues. "A humble existence sustained by the blood and the land is a wholesome existence. We shy from the world beyond the hills and for that, we have preserved the integrity of the vison that our forefathers sought to instill. Let us give thanks to their bravery and their apparition, and all that has blossomed of it. Let us pray together over this union—"

"Meyrick!" I wake to shaking, shouting, and Leroy's anxious appearance. "Meyrick, wake the hell up!"

"What is it, Leroy?"

"Meyrick, we're in a bad way!" He releases my shoulders and stands above me.

I'm initially dumbfounded. It comes back to me as quickly as the vision of my wedding day is retreating. The recollection of the lantern-carrying trespassers coupled with his worry-smeared expression nearly slaps a smile on my face.

"What does that mean, Leroy? Do explain."

"Meyrick, I done got skunk-drunk last night and can't find my truck keys."

Repositioning myself on the divan, I watch him pace anxiously. "Don't you have a spare set?"

"That ain't the point, woman!" Hand to his forehead, he stares at me, waiting for answers.

"Leroy, I've never once seen you bring your keys indoors. You've always left them in the ignition."

"Don't you think I know that? Your dumbass can't drive no truck and the damn thing ain't worth the trouble to steal. Someone done took them keys, Meyrick!" His voice trembles under his distress.

"Oh." I stand. "Even creatures of habit are only creatures."

"What the hell does that mean?"

"I'm certain the keys are either in this house or dropped in the mud near your truck just waiting to be found."

He paces at me a bit longer before bolting from the sitting room. There isn't a piece of me that believes the keys to his truck were drunkenly dropped in a mud puddle or misplaced among cookery and other countertop items in the kitchen. The lights were real. People were here and whoever they were, they wish to ensure that Leroy remains stationary.

I walk calmly to the kitchen and peer out the screen-door to watch him scrambling through the floorboards of his tattered truck. He knows, and knowing he knows is the sweetest nectar.

"Dammit, Meyrick! If I found out you done took them keys!" His muffled words come through the open truck doors.

"Leroy," I call from inside. "Have you checked the barn?"

The search halts. His head appears over the roof of the truck. "You…do you think I oughtta?"

With every ounce of composure, I make my way to join him. "I do. You're so certain someone came to this farm to take your keys, but why? What motive might there be?"

His head shakes frantically. "No. There's…there's no way in hell. Don't no one know but you and me."

"For peace of mind, let us visit the barn. Then we'll find your truck keys and I'll prepare breakfast."

His muttering is mostly inaudible as I trail him to the smallest of the barns. The farmyard is dappled in drops of dew reflecting the morning's rays like thousands of tiny eyes staring up at me. The area surrounding the barn resembles a moat. If there were people here searching around the buildings, their footprints were washed away. We move alongside the barn between the water and saturated wood until we reach the rear of it.

The doves perching on the barbed wire are sent skyward as his shrieks fill the atmosphere.

"He's gone! Someone done took him!"

I haven't the words to calm Leroy. The makeshift grave among garbage now lies robbed and flooded—a muddy, miniature pond.

"Them people! Them ones!" He turns his rage to me, pointing a furious finger as he steps in my direction.

"What?"

"Them hands! Them hired hands!" He stumbles toward me.

"No. They're gone, Leroy. They left. I told you they left."

I'm caged between the rotting barn and his rotting frown. "Who was they!"

"Leroy, they left. I assure you this wasn't them. That Antonio—"

"I kill't that bastard too! Came at me askin' a heap of no good questions…" He pauses. "You…you said he was snoopin' round the farm? You said that he was lookin' around here!"

"I did."

"He knew, Meyrick. He knew and said something before I could get him in the ground!"

"Said something to whom though, Leroy?" I ask as he storms away. "Who are these people?"

10.

"Hurry, Meyrick!" Jennet's giggle from outside the bedroom door is one more reason to smile.

"Come in, you silly thing. Kaleb is due back in the hour."

Within the McCormick home I'm neither family nor enemy. Kaleb's parents greet me pleasantly, yet kind smiles lie under wrathful eyes. I feel I'm tolerated best if I remain stowed away, and so I'm typically self-confined to this small bedroom Kaleb and I share until our home is complete within the Community.

"I have it!" Jennet announces softly as she produces a glimmering and flimsy piece of literature.

"Jennet. Have you no shame? Your parents hate me as it is. If they find this—"

"They don't hate you, Meyrick. They're adapting." She grins. "Shall we?"

Multiple aspects of these contraband reading pieces, featuring scandalously clad, gorgeous women peering at us from the front cover, evokes an evergreen envy. The Cosmopolitan.

The brown-haired beauty featured on the April 1973 edition appears to be staring into my soul. She poses next to words that have my face flushing warm as I read them. The flower-speckled garment she wears appears cold and uncomfortable. I'm unenvious of her garb— the colossal, metal ornaments adorning her ears and wrist, reflecting the light like meadow streams in the morning. I'm left unimpressed by the ruby-painted pout of her lips and matching red fingernails...so unnaturally odd.

Her gaze—it lacks the slightest indication of

remorse as she displays her arms and the valley of her breasts. The strength and power behind her decision to have her photograph taken leaves me longing for more than a monthly taste smuggled in from the outside. Her beauty may be as evident as an iris in full bloom, yet it is her strength I crave.

We quietly thumb through the pages—scanning over colorfully dressed men and women boasting beautiful smiles. "I want this, Jennet."

"What?"

"I want to walk into a library and read the literature of my choosing, and stay for the length of my choosing, and do so without an escort. I want…" I shrug in frustration before tapping a picture with the back of my hand, "…this."

"To drink from funny-looking glasses with boys?" Jennet asks curiously.

"No. Look at her. Look at them. They're all friends and there isn't anything sinful or damningly inappropriate about it. They're simply young and enjoying it, and rather than waiting to be summoned for fresh liquor, the girls are in the thick of it, enjoying it as if they're equals."

I feel Jennet's eyes on the side of my face as I continue staring at the splayed images. "How would that be possible, Meyrick? It's fiction."

"But is it? Lewder fiction lives on the shelves of the Community Library, unscathed, and available for reading. Explain to me why, Jennet, if this is fictitious, it is forbidden."

The bathroom door opens. "Don't you open the front door for no one, and I mean, nobody!"

I only nod. All but my face is submerged, and my

nodding head sends milky ripples through the bathwater.

"What the…" He steps into the bathroom. "Well, well." He retrieves his magazine from the closed lid of the commode with a wolfish grin. "Meyrick, I see we got somethin' in common."

Breathe… "There was an article—"

"That's what we all say," he hoots. "Ain't no need for being shy with it. None at all."

"You're leaving me here…knowing they're coming?"

His chuckle fills the confined space once more. "If I took you anywhere it'd look like I was trying to run, now wouldn't it?"

His exit has questions coursing. If Leroy fails to return, do I flee to the barns to rot among them? Do I remain motionless and wait for vengeance to surround me? What is freedom without strength?

Dried and dressed, I make my way through the home, ensuring each window is locked and both doors are secured. It's an odd thing, barring myself within a home when nearly my entire life I've wanted nothing but to flee the one I resided in.

There's an uncontrollable urge to pace the floor and chew the rough and jagged parts of my fingernails away. The day drains slowly from the house.

I've never feared the night or what dwells within it. Yet, I'm disturbed knowing this night might bring with it something more sinister than Leroy.

The last of the orange hue dissolves on the walls and ceiling as the sun sinks in the trees.

From the kitchen the tea kettle screams. Just as I turn my gaze from the sitting room window, the glass is assaulted from the outside with a loud thud.

"Oh!" Whatever struck the window did so with incredible force, yet the glass remains intact.

Slowly, shaking, I move closer to examine. *Nothing.* But then, center of the pane, I eye tiny plumages secured to the glass and waving about in place.

A glance toward the ground reveals a pathetic sight, indeed. A broken raven, perhaps a crow, flails and flops about on the ground just below the window.

Without hesitancy I race toward the door before pausing—knob in hand. *Is this trickery?* Outside, I move more methodically in the direction of the cackling creature.

My eyes beg to glance elsewhere—as if I'm approaching a massacre.

"Are you real?" My soft whisper neither calms nor further riles the bird. It continues somersaulting as I kneel to it. "Don't...don't be frightened."

She rests on her back beneath me—talons curled and heavenward, glaring up as if she's accepted her looming end. "You aren't here with me, are you?"

My trembling hand nears her face and is painfully snipped by her impressively powerful beak. "Oh, my word. You are here!"

As I find my footing, the bird does too. She hops twice before returning beautifully to the sky and soaring beyond a silo in the distance.

A thin stream of blood adorns the back of my hand and middle finger like lacey red ribbon.

"She was here...she was real." I bear the painful proof of her existence.

Outside the home I'm surprisingly blessed with an odd sense of well-being. There's no longing to pace and gnaw at my fingers. The realization comes swiftly—to return indoors and lock myself in tight would equate to a freed rat reentering the ghastly trap I sprung it from.

The woodlands, with their snaking, starlit trails, call to me once more. I race barefoot into them as naturally as the raven did the sky.

11.

"Your mind isn't a sketchpad, Jennet. You won't be able to erase this or tear it away once it's there."

We lean on the west wall of the McCormick home, staring into the mouth of the forest.

"If it were a sketchpad or some canvas…my mind, I could memorialize this morning on the back of my eyelids in exquisite detail." She turns to me, grinning. "I assure you, this is nothing I'll want to tear away."

I find the chill to her voice perplexing. Similar to the perils my mind conjures while swimming in the lake and my feet paddle through cooler water below. "Okay then. Let's be on our way."

I walk timidly behind her into the welcoming forest. Beneath the blanket of branches the heat amplifies immediately. So heavy is the air that drawing it in feels no longer involuntary.

"Jennet," I call. "Jennet, may I ask you something?"

She slows her pace while I gather the courage to ask the question. "You said…you said, he came to you, once more," I stammer as she turns to me. "The day it happened, you said—"

"I'm aware of what I said, Meyrick. What exactly is it you wish to ask me?" Expressionless, she moves forward.

"How many times, Jennet, did he rape you?"

Her head shakes, eyes close as she turns from me. "I stopped…I was twelve when…and…I stopped counting." Her words fade into her tears.

"What? Jennet. The entire time? You never…you didn't tell me—"

"He was my uncle, Meyrick. What was I supposed to say?"

I haven't the words to comfort her. Tears stream, yet she remains rigidly poised like a crying sculpture.

"Jennet." I ease closer. "We could have prayed. I would have been there with you when you told the Church."

"Oh, I prayed, Meyrick. No longer." She looks to the emerald canopy above us. "I prayed each time he collected me. I prayed, watching my tummy swell with what was his." Her gaze falls heavy on mine—cold and tortured. "I prayed as my father left me bruised and bleeding, my belly bludgeoned, and my bastard, no bigger than a sparrow, wrapped in soiled rags until I was sturdy enough to dig the little demon a grave behind the hen-house."

"Jennet—"

"I pray no more, Meyrick."

Her history is my own—I remain stunned and motionless as it crumbles and reconstructs in seconds while she vanishes calmly into the thicket.

It's an odd thing, trailing my best-friend—her beautiful smile and boisterous laugh, and only now knowing the cross she carries.

Our pace matches one another's as we walk silently for several minutes. The area appears remarkably unlike it did before. The thick vegetation has me wondering if we've lost our way. Just as I'm opening my mouth to enquire, the hint of decay assures me we're near.

"Wait. Jennet, just wait."

Sweat and apprehension adorn her face as she turns my way. "Meyrick, this is mine. I want this—"

"I love you, Jennet!" I embrace her. The radiating heat is nearly unbearable, yet I hug her still. "I love you so much."

"I know this, Meyrick."

We decouple as I rest my hands atop her shoulders.

"Jennet, I didn't know…and I'm so sorry for that, but I need you to know that you are important—"

"Meyrick—"

"You will hear me, Jennet! You are important. There were days I couldn't and wouldn't have been able to rise if not for your friendship. You are important to me. You're important to this world, and not…not because you are a wife, or future wife or someone's daughter. You are important as you are. You are somebody and you are perfect, and I need—"

"Meyrick—"

"I need you to look at me and tell me you know that! Tell me you know you are more than what he did to you."

"I know this, Meyrick. Do you?" She takes my hand. "Who are you convincing here?"

"What? Jennet, I know you are loved. I know I too am loved by you and my husband." I squeeze her hand. "Once we leave here, our true value—"

"We talk of leaving this place and our families like there are options beyond our lives here, but without a plan we might as well be talking about the moon, Meyrick."

I merely nod. "Okay. We'll plan then."

"Okay then. We shall plan. For now, understand why I need this." She smiles quaintly before turning.

"Jennet…look at them." As we approach what is left of her monster, we find him being picked over by

beautiful ravens and magpies. "They're gorgeous!"

Jennet nears the birds and torn clothing of Samuel. The majority of the marauders call out in protest of our presence as they take to the trees or the sky. The area is pungently permeated, and the cavity of the body is writhing in tiny white pearls—maggots.

"Look at him!" Jennet exclaims with a grin.

I find I'm entranced, inching closer to the oblivious fledglings.

"Meyrick, do you hear that? I think someone is over there."

Her warning comes just as I'm reaching for one of the smaller of the birds. Frightened, it turns from its putrid feast with a razor beak to lacerate my curious hand.

"No!" Feet flailing, horizontal, my eyes open to peculiar surroundings. Soggy soil is my pillow. Bits of blue of sky play peekaboo in the swaying greenery far above me—a kaleidoscope with no rhyme or pattern.

"Hello? Jennet?" Sitting forward sends small twigs and other debris tumbling from my clothing and hair. My mind is fogged over. I'm filthy and completely confused by the situation at hand—*hand*!

"Ah!" My hand bears the wound I received the evening prior while attempting to assist the misguided bird. Only now do I notice the excruciating pain arising from the gash. The blood pouring from the small wound pools in my lap to reflect my horrified expression.

"Stop…stop!" Pressing my thump to the pulsating cut only aggravates the injury further—I am bleeding at an alarming rate.

As I stand to run, my world goes dark and I nearly

crash once more to the forest floor. Deep, slow inhalations help to regain stability as I walk in the direction of a small stream.

Cool and blood-drenched, my gown clings to my thighs. Small cobblestones lead up to the rushing water's entrance. Falling to my knees, I begin vigorously rinsing the cut the bird inflicted on my hand with cool creek water.

Like climbing vines, the pain expands from my hand and up my arm—wrapping it tight in excruciation.

There is nothing to do but toss my face skyward and scream—disperse the agony among the trees. An idea of ending it *all* instantly within the waters before me is immediately quelled when, to my surprise, the pain ceases.

With my gaze transfixed still to the sky and trees above me, I lift my trembling hand to my face. The initial relief of finding my skin woundless and unbloodied is swiftly exchanged with sheer terror and confusion.

The back of my hand bears only a slender scar inflicted by a young raven years prior while with Jennet at the grave of Samuel. The lack of injury leaves only one conclusion; no raven barreled into the sitting-room window the previous evening. She didn't snip my hand as I attempted to assist her. Vivid as my memory may be, I never watched her take flight to the night and hide behind the silo. She was never there.

Like the snow in late March, my mind is leaving. Further evidence of this comes as I look to my blood-free attire. Only fresh water wets my clothing.

I remain seated before the stream. Singing birds, wind-swept trees—the forest's sonata is only noise now. My personal world—alone with my thoughts, has been an unwavering sanctuary and I'm witnessing that reduce rapidly.

My gown is hung to dry on a branch while I piece together the previous evening. *To the back and to the brink.* No. As I look upon my surroundings, contemplating what comes next, I find the reality is that nothing is sustainable.

Ravens—dark, enduring, enchantingly beautiful with an ability to leave at will. Rationalizing the fascination's fueling is easy. They are everything I'm not. I'm delicate, dependent, and my blonde beauty has done little but cause me misery. However, there is no rationalization for my mind's bending of reality other than madness. Given my grave circumstances, psychosis is a damning element to add to the equation.

The sun leisurely tiptoes overhead. Her warmth is welcome, and her location is my only indication of time.

The fog has somewhat lifted from my boggy brain, yet I find myself fearful to glance about my surroundings, fearful of seeing what is not there, or even being assaulted by those imaginings.

After leaving the home last night, I delved deep into the woodland. As my belly grumbles, I'm reminded I'm likely a great distance from sustenance. The ground beneath me isn't scattered with acorns or any other edibles.

An hour passes before the gown is dry enough to slip in to. Once dressed, I scan the area once more for anything that appears appetizing. Nothing does.

I meander about the trails as if I'll stumble across an option growing wildly somewhere. There are no other possibilities or resources available. As midday settles directly atop me, my ears hear the howling of a devil through the forest. Leroy is calling my name.

"Meyrick!"

I'm unsure if I'm more baffled by the fact that he's traveled so deep into the wood to collect me, or that I'm mildly enthused that he has.

He continues calling. He's an option, the only option. As I walk in the direction of his voice, it becomes clear I'm a creature of the present. I live in the now and thrive on those scattered bits of bliss from my past. There is no future beyond tomorrow—beyond necessity. If notions of escaping this existence and idyllic outcomes featuring independence…books and warm tea had any legitimacy, I would not be walking back to him once more. I am no raven. His stumbling, cursing image coming into view through the foliage attests that.

"Leroy?"

As we approach one another I'm taken aback by his alarming appearance. He peers at me through slits for eyes, frowns at me through splitting lips. So swollen and bruised are his facial features that he is almost unrecognizable.

"What…what happened to—"

"What the fuck are you doin' out here? I told you to stay indoors and keep it locked up!"

"I'm…I'm sorry, Leroy. I was so frightened."

He stares—his swollen face is nearly incapable of expression. "Let's get," he mumbles before shaking his head and turning.

"Leroy."

"What?"

"I just want to say thank you for coming so far to find me. I know you've walked a great deal."

He turns to me once more. "What in the hell are you talkin' about, you lunatic? The house ain't but a couple hundred meters up the way. Did you eat some of them crazy mushrooms while you was out here or something? Hurry the hell up. I'm hungry as hell and you need a bath."

12.

There's something in his embrace, some safe-harbor—it unclenches my jaw and untenses my shoulders. He makes breathing easier.

I loathe most creatures with beards…the way they passively glance and smirk simultaneously…the way they take. Our world is their bounty and I'm one of the pretty faces scurrying about the spoils, collecting what they desire and delivering it with a courteous smile and diverted gaze.

Kaleb's beard is stubble at best but that isn't what defers my disdain. Our gaze remains connected as I divulge my dreams of a life with days spent crafting poetry, sipping tea, and devouring novels—novels housed on shelves in my own home.

I witness the joy slide from his face like sheets of snow from warming tin roofs when the subject matter transitions to childhoods and life outside the bedroom we share. He loves me. I feel a rooted connection similar to that I shared with my mother prior to her departure…or disappearance. Similar to that with Jennet. I could unlace my mind and expose my every thought to the man before me and I feel he'd only kiss me, blushingly.

He is my family.

Side by side and to each other, our faces pressed to the sheets beneath us, he mutters a word. One word. "Idaho," with a grin.

"What?"

"Idaho."

Propping myself on my elbow in the shambled bedding, I look down on him—sleepy-eyed with a wild man's hair. "I heard you, Kaleb. What does that mean?"

He chuckles into his pillow. "It's an American state."

"Don't be silly. I know every American state and capital."

His boyish smile is half hidden in the pillow as he eyes me playfully. I marvel the idea of that pillow capturing his laughter in the early morning hours. What I would pay to rest my head in those blisses.

"Kaleb, what about it?"

"Potatoes," he says chipperly.

I smirk. "Are you hungry? What would you like with your pota—"

"Let's leave here for Idaho. Let's farm potatoes." The bedsprings shift and squeak as he sits and crosses his legs. There's an intensity to his smile that assures me the proposal is authentic, and yet I find myself cynical.

"Kaleb, such things shouldn't be joked about. You know I long to leave the Community one day."

He takes my hand in his. "Meyrick McCormick, my beautiful wife, I am asking you to leave with me, abandon our homes and families for a foreign land and the unknown. Will you leave the Community, Alberta...Canada...and become a poor potato farmer with me?"

My eyes instantly flood. "Kaleb, I want nothing more!"

"Oh yeah?"

"Yes! I want a life rich in potatoes! Potatoes for each meal, even!"

His tears streak too.

"When? When will this happen, Kaleb?"

He fills his chest to the brink. "Henry comes at week's end to collect the saleable goods and bring pharmaceuticals. We're to be ready to depart when he leaves."

"What? So soon?" I press either temple as if my head is physically expanding with the information.

"Yes. So soon. He won't be back before the snow returns and Alberta wraps us up again. If we don't depart before the house is complete, my parents will be liable for the expense of the build. Now is the only time."

"Kaleb...how? Where will we go?"

He grins. "It is planned. American crop farms readily hire cheap work hands. We'll have a place, Meyrick."

I feel the pulse in my eyes as I stare at his beaming face. "And Jennet? We can't—"

"Even if I have to drag her, screaming. We're leaving. The three of us are to be filthy, potato farming fools!"

I hug him—squeeze him. "Kaleb, I've never heard more beautiful words. America...I can't imagine!"

"You won't have to, Meyrick. It's happening." As we decouple, I witness the excitement in his eyes. "This is only the start. Can't you see it? We'll have our own piece of it all one day. Our own farm. And you may collect every book in print, even if it means we cover the walls of our little home in shelves from floor to ceiling!"

"Oh, Kaleb..."

"Your cat...your tea...and your little window to gaze out of while writing your poetry. That will be our

future. We just have to plant it. We have to get a bit dirty."

"Am I dreaming? Is this real, Kaleb?"

"I said I wanted a life with you, Meyrick. Let's go get it."

"What the fuck are you cryin' for? Ain't like you're the one busted up all to hell."

Leroy enters the sitting room. A washcloth, spotted in burgundy, is pressed to his oozing facial wounds.

"I'm sorry, Leroy," I mumble from the divan.

"Would you stop apologizing? That shit gets annoying." There is minimal movement from his split and distended lips as he spews his hatred.

"I'm…yes."

He wanders to the window, walking achily with a widened gait. I watch him, watching the dirt road as if he's expecting it to produce something other than dust. His actions say what his words will not. Something is coming. For the first time I feel an odd connection. He and I are both caged with keys.

"Leroy."

He says nothing, blinks entirely too many times, and continues looking through the window.

"Leroy, please."

"What, Meyrick!"

"Tell me, Leroy. Who was Ricardo? What happened to you and who still do we have to fear?"

"Dammit, Meyrick!" His breath fogs the glass just inches from his face. Silence takes the room. I dare not enquire further, but then there's no need to. To my surprise, he turns from the window. "Ricardo was a dealer of sorts. Anything from them fightin' roosters to that marijuana…" He attempts to smile but it is hindered by his injuries. "And then there's the real assets."

His pause has me nodding, prompting him to continue.

"Ricardo, and others like him, line their billfolds by delivering farmhands, ditch-digging fools and occasionally…pretty little things like you."

"I came here free willing, Leroy, to work and build a better life."

"Ya did. Didn't quite go as planned, did it, sugar-puss?"

"Objectify me all you like. I'll never be property."

"That don't mean it didn't cost nothin' to get ya here," he snaps.

Confusion compiles. "Leroy, what debt is there? What danger?"

"Ah, Meyrick, it's like…well, it's like you done chopped off a thorny piece of some weed, you know?" He moves closer to me—the tone of his voice softening with his attempt at being philosophical. "And now ya done left me no choice but to cut a few more of them thorns because they keep stickin' in my side." He shakes his sausage of a finger at me, the way the church leaders would when driving their message. "But the thing with it…with this weed in our yard…we don't got no clue how deep them roots go, or how big they get." He shrugs. "We might get good and stuck, or we might keep on clippin' with no issue." He nods affirmatively.

"Stuck? Leroy, we could flee. Why stay here?"

"Like I done said, woman, that weed is in *our* yard. His arms cross confidently. They resemble dimpled dough where they link to his trunk as he stands before me in an altered, sleeveless shirt. "How's that for analogy or, like a, metaphorical or what have ya?"

I set the quilt aside and stand. "Your face. They could have killed you, Leroy."

"Ah, Meyrick. Don't you go acting like that concerns you none. Neither of the ol' boys who put this hurt on me died smiling. Somethin' for the books, if you ask me." He slaps his thigh before leaving me to my worries.

I find his mid-morning presence within the home most intrusive. This weed he speaks of has annihilated any surviving concept of normalcy.

Hanging the linen on the line takes unreasonably longer than average. I'm nearly tempted to unpin each item and rehang the entire wash in an effort to remain outdoors. Then I hear humming. Beautiful, melodic purring floats over the yard and evolves to words—lovely singing…*Spanish*. It comes from the smallest of the barns, *the raided grave*.

"Anna?" I mutter. There's a physical fluttering in my chest, a tickle almost. "Could it be?"

Three steps into my sprint I remind myself of Leroy's presence—ever watching like a hungry hawk. Briskly yet discreetly, I walk toward the barn…toward the voice.

"Anna?" I call out as I push through the door. My gaze rests on an empty bed of hay.

"Emily?"

"Oh!" I leap and spin like a spooked barn cat. "My…oh my word!"

"So sorry. So sorry for frightening you." A fresh-faced Anna is a welcome sight.

"Where on earth have you been? Where is Q? I've been…I've been worried, and…and I thought you were gone forever."

"Gone forever? No. Our stories. They are not over. You know? You remember?"

"Anna," I take her hand, "where is Q? People are angry. You just left without telling me."

She pulls from me. "Q is gathering. We have much to protect now." Her petite hands rub atop her abdomen lovingly. "So much to protect."

"What? You're expecting?"

"Pregnant? Si."

Her face, the way she looks adoringly toward her belly, still flat under her hands, I could slap her. "Are you insane?"

"Emily?"

"What do you plan to do, birth a newborn like a barnyard beast in the dead of winter? Why would you do this, Anna?"

Her smile dies. "You so angry with me, Emily."

"Yes! I can't…this isn't something I can help you with."

"Help me? No, we don't need your help," she replies with a soured expression and confident tone. "We don't need nothing from you. You know my story, but what have you learned from it?" She heads out of the back of the barn before I can respond. I follow her, longing for answers, craving her companionship.

"Anna, I need you take into the consideration the gravity of the—"

"You see?" She interrupts me, pointing proudly toward the metal gate as my eyes transition to the light, and to horror. "We take care of our self."

"Anna!" Mouth agape, I stare in shock. The metal stock gate acts as a crucifix, holding a lifeless and bloodied man upright. His arm appears painfully twisted and malformed within the bars of the gate, detaining the deceased.

"For you." She presents a bloodied blade.

"What have you done?" I mutter, taking the weapon.

"Protecting my family…and you, Emily. I heard his noises, so I ran here to see him tangled up. Little moth in a web." Like a painter admiring her work on an easel—arms crossed and standing with a tilt, her stare glued to the lifeless mess before us, she continues. "This trapped man was no man. Crying." She giggles and mimics the action of her hand thrusting the blade into the man's chest. "One stabbing and no more. So much bleeding."

"Anna—"

"Do you have something to eat? I'm hungry, Emily. We both are hungry." She unconcernedly rubs her belly before turning from the body.

"Anna, you can't just kill people. There are consequences."

She pauses, her back still to me. "Emily…I'm tired of hurting. So are you." She continues to the barn. "Please, I'm hungry. Q will be too."

13.

To me, their love is nothing to envy, the couples of the community. I've grown up surrounded by it and never wanted it. They all look the same—remind me of a picture I saw of some town in Mexico. Pretty, little adobe homes…identical, bland in tone with a fragile appearance as though a good, hard rain could wash them away.

We're different, Kaleb and me. Our foundation is each other, rather than the Community. He is my strength, and haunted as our structure may be, it never will wash away.

The idea of uprooting isn't so unnerving as there isn't much to uproot. Each hour that passes is one less under the watchful eye of my father. Whatever hardships may come, I'm ready for the next chapter.

Two dresses and undergarments are folded before me. I'll pack just as lightly for Kaleb. If we're to escape into the night, we'll need to go lightly. There isn't much to pack, which is for the best. I'd leave most my memories here if I could. The idea of starting anew as Meyrick McCormick, with dirt under her nails, is as invigorating as fresh Spring air.

A ruckus moving up the staircase has me snatching up the folded clothing.

"Meyrick!" Jennet startles me, rushing through the bedroom door. "Meyrick, they found him. They've found Samuel."

The porcelain cup falls from my grasp to the linoleum and snares my attention. It remains intact.

Death is an inescapable cloud. It hangs stanch throughout the home, assailing my senses and dampening my wounded psyche. There isn't an amount of mentholated jelly I can apply inside my nostrils to alleviate it.

Anna wasn't there when I left the plate of food atop the splintered stool in the barn. I didn't search her out or even call for her. Not with death dangling just outside the backdoor of the barn.

The thunderous snoring from the bedroom ceases. He is awake.

"Meyrick," he mumbles, summoning me.

From the bedroom doorway my insides tangle and constrict like trumpet vine at the thought of his touch…his breath, as I look upon him in the sheets. I pray he doesn't beckon me to bed.

"What in god's name is that smell?"

"Pardon?"

"Did a rat crawl up in the wall and croak?" He kicks his thin legs over the side of the bed and stares at the wall. "It smells like a whore's cunt in here."

I'm relieved the odor isn't something residual in my nose, altering my sense of smell or even some hallucination of my senses.

"I'll light a candle, Leroy."

"Wait," he snaps as I turn. "What business did you have down in the cellar earlier?"

"I beg your pardon?"

"The cellar. I heard the rope creakin' and the door slam. What was you doin' down there?"

I completely despise that dank, dusty, and crumbling place. The walls speckled with spiders' eyes and the corners housing an abundance of shadows to cloak scaly untouchables, enameled and slithering from sight. I'd annihilate it from my memory if possible. It must have been Anna or Q.

"The smell, Leroy. I was investigating the source of the smell."

He only chuckles. His laughter moves through the entire bed, yet nothing is happy here. "Investigate no further than that slop in your britches."

"Leroy!"

"Oh," he coughs out. "I'm kiddin' ya. Too delicate."

His idiocies are the least of my concerns. If Anna or Q are meddling in the bowels of this dilapidated home I need to know why.

"Heat a skillet. Bacon might hide the rat-stink," Leroy calls from the room.

"Yes, Leroy. I'll be starting the wash soon. If you plan to shower with hot water, you might do so now."

Hygienically challenged, Leroy is never anxious to bathe even after a long day in the fields. I'm nearly surprised to hear the shower water running and echoing down the drain.

Atypical, still I waste no time. Out the front and to the peeling and spongy, wooden cellar door, alive with moss and petite vines. It groans and moans as I lift on the slick metal handle, opening the nightmarish hole to tiny scattering things. Rising like heat from cookery, a putrid perfume engulfs me from the depths of the cellar. This is no rat. This isn't even one-hundred rats. This is death in a grander form.

After finding my breath, I find the fortitude to take the first step inside and descend against my better judgment. Natural light guides my footing and I dare not touch the web-draped walls on either side. So thick is the air with the ripe taste of decay that my teeth and the roof of my mouth are glazed in it.

The shadows here aren't welcoming—they mean to keep things tucked away like an angry lockbox full of gruesome answers. Even the shadows, however, are useless at hiding this.

Death is horrible at keeping secrets. There's always traces. There's always tears of ambitious loved ones, hellbent on resolution. And even if it isn't witnessed, death typically leaves something to seep, bloat, and rot.

"Goddamn you, Meyrick! I fuckin' knew it!" Leroy's voice reverberates off the walls, gnawing its way into my skull from behind while I stare at the swollen corpse in the corner. Rusted pipes along the cellar walls still hum with rushing water. He fooled me into thinking he was bathing.

"Who is this, Meyrick?"

"I don't know, Ler—"

"You know what his last words to me was?" His question runs along my cheek from behind.

"Wh…who, Leroy? This man? I don't know this—"

"You know who I'm talkin' bout, you lyin' whore." He inches closer. "He said he was ready to leave you."

"Stop!" Face to face, within striking distance, I raise my chin and welcome whatever he's offering. "I don't know what happened here, Leroy! I haven't been down here since…"

He thrusts his belly into me, sandwiching me between him and the crawling wall behind. "Go on."

"You know when. I had nothing to do with this gentleman's demise. I would tell you if I had."

Like his smut literature plastered aside the commode, he studies my expression intensely until he's satisfied. "Okay then, where'd the asshole come from?"

I can only shrug, mouth agape as I look past Leroy to the dead man in the corner. He's garbed in a laborer's attire and all the filth of this awful place. "I don't know, Leroy. I've never seen him before in my life."

He meanders closer. "Oh," he yelps sharply. "Well, goddamn." Nostrils flared, brow furrowed, he peers down. "This is the work of a black widow."

His statement has my glance tracing the sunlit tinseled webbing of the stairwell for penny-sized assassins boasting blood-red bellies.

"Spiders?" I ask with a quivering voice.

"What? No. My god, you're ignorant. Come see." He motions me toward him.

"You see that?" He follows up as I approach. "Tell me you don't know, but this bastard got's his trousers undid and he's cut all to hell. Black widow. A bitch."

The poor fellow at me feet is certainly in an awful way. The worn, navy-blue button up shirt is stained with black, sappy blood.

"You took a blade to his back like a coward, Meyrick."

"What? No, Leroy—"

"You're a cheap glass of whisky. Hard to choke down and easy to replace." Anger grips his voice. "Piss you out in the morning like it's nothing."

"Leroy, I'm telling you the truth."

"This boy was a decent fella. He was one of Ricardo's, but he had more sense than the rest combined. Wasn't no need for this bullshit. This here was a good man."

He kneels to the man, shaking his head. "Coulda' been settled some other way, Meyrick."

"Leroy, you're not hearing me—"

"Hear me, woman!" He stands, electrified, the back of his hand sends me stumbling backwards, grasping my face. "You done went too far with this one!"

Stunned, I remain silent as he wheezes before me, red-faced with raging eyes.

"This man has callused his hands in the same fields as me for years. Wasn't no need for this bullshit. This could have been settled with words." His mouth forms a quivering, angry upside-down U. "I got me a grave to dig. A proper grave. I'm fixin' on diggin' two."

He studies my expression, but I give him nothing. Vacancy.

"Get out of here, Meyrick. You disgust me."

***

The trouble with tin roofs is they capture the sound of every pelting raindrop. Every clang, ting, thud, and ring, resounds and masks anything else. Squeezing Kaleb's hand, I stare toward the bedroom ceiling from the bed.

There's rumbling within the kitchen, something other than dinner is brewing. A sea of passive voices drowning in the downpour. Occasionally an impassioned plea will resonate above the monotony, yet the words are indistinguishable.

We've been casually confined here, Kaleb and I, and Jennet to her room. Hours pass slowly, flooding our minds with ill thoughts and worst-case scenarios. Palms clasped, moist with sweat and fear, breath choppy with dread at the thought of being dragged from the home, through the mud, and into the clutches of persecution, we wait.

The bedroom door opens, snatching my breath.

Silent as a serpent, Jennet slips in—her complexion a pale, anxious gray.

"Jennet," Kaleb whispers, sitting forward on the bed. "You'll have us all under the reeds."

"Kaleb..." Her tears flow. "Kaleb, I'm petrified." She moves to the bed cautiously—tiptoeing along the squeaking hardwoods before falling to her knees at bedside. "I've prayed. I've begged the heavens to swallow me up. Why am I unanswered?"

He takes her trembling hands. "Jennet, we don't know what they know. Perhaps we're not suspected at all."

"You know that isn't true, Kaleb. We'll be face down in the dirt in two days' time." An electric tension has her expression jolting. Her lips, eyelids, and nostrils twitch randomly as she teeters on the verge of utter collapse. "I don't want to die, Kaleb."

He leans to her and grasps her trembling shoulders. His whispering lips to her ear quells her shivering in seconds.

The room is stagnated in a dreadful distress that is inescapable, and yet he's calmed her with his words.

The door opens to loud boots and silent stares.

There's a helpless look about Kaleb and Jennet's parents' faces that assures me our worries were well-founded. In front of them are Edgar Dunham, Stewart Iverson, and my father.

"Samuel McCormick was bludgeoned to death," my father's voice fills the room like candlelight in a pitch-black pantry. "His remains bear the evidence of that." He enters the room. His gaze floats just above us...his hands folded behind his back. "A young witness, most respectable in the eyes of the Church, followed

you...ladies, to the deceased, where she overheard damming conversation."

"Father—"

"Silence, murderess."

"No!" Kaleb leaps from the bed. "You will not disrespect my wife or sister when it was I that struck him down."

"Kaleb!" I interject.

"No, Meyrick. This fiend is hellbent on your misery because he can't see you. He sees only your mother...you're an extension of the woman who fled and left him like the miserable wretch he is."

"You ungrateful heathen." My father steps to Kaleb, trembling with fury. "You will perish under my reed. You won't arise. Do you hear me?"

I stand aside my husband. "No. He isn't responsible."

Kaleb's grasp on my hand is instant and nearly painful.

"Are you claiming your husband is a liar, Meyrick?" my father questions.

"I'm not lying," Kaleb mutters through gritting teeth.

"Then you shall be tossed to the dirt and the reeds will make short work of your thin skin just before the good Lord casts his final—"

"There is a process, Father!" I interrupt, silencing the room momentarily.

"Very well, Daughter. The process begins now. Edgar, Stewart, take the younger Mr. McCormick under arrest to the Church for interrogation."

Kaleb seems to physically deflate. His breath leaves him, his head lowers, and his eyes pool as the men take both arms and lead him away.

I couldn't hear what he'd whispered in Jennet's ear just moments prior...brotherly words had soothed her worries by offering to bear her cross. I can't hear him now as they take him away. He may have said I love you or may simply be crying out in fear. His words are muffled by the rains. That's the trouble with tin roofs.

14.

Perhaps his back grew too achy or perhaps his hands trembled without a glass in them for so long. Regardless, only one mounded gravesite adorns the furthest piece of the yard, quite fittingly tucked among a boneyard of tractors and antique farm equipment. I'll die another day, perhaps.

Leroy bathes now. Removing the remnants of the cellar fellow left him no choice but to wash away the foul rancidness of the deed.

A soft breeze coaxes death from the home and out of the propped windows—each of them held open with wooden spoons, tools and other trinkets. A boiling pot of water and mentholated jelly with tea leaves has masked the stench in the kitchen entirely, although, it draws tears instantly upon entering.

It is asinine to ponder why she killed him. Assuming more bodies might accumulate, however, is certainly something to think on. Leroy won't tolerate another murderous transaction. If he stumbles on the barn fellow or even some other bled-out wretch, he'll end me.

"Meyrick!" his voice tears from the bathroom.

In the sitting room, I glance out the window toward the dying dogwood, hoping my name won't be repeated. He summons me once more.

So swollen is the bathroom door that it is nearly stuck-tight with condensation. It jolts and shudders as I enter to retreating steam.

I find Leroy beneath the cascading water; the shower curtain is open, and the floor is pooling.

"I'm gonna need some help finishin' this," he says,

pointing to his erection as the water parts over it.

"I don't feel well, Leroy."

"I imagine you don't after what you done. You don't gotta be sunny-side-up for decent handy work. Tug a lug, woman."

I've heard this request hundreds of times and it's certainly the least repulsive, yet the entirety of the day's events has me genuinely queasy and seeing his manhood, aggressive with excitement under his swollen, hairy belly, only exacerbates my nausea.

I fall to the commode and purge the coffee I'd just previously drank.

"Oh, now. Come on, Meyrick. Just like milkin' a cow 'cept ya ain't gonna get the yield…well hell, I dunno. Been so long—"

"There's…there's another body," I choke out, echoing into the toilet bowl.

"What the fuck did you just say?"

Warm droplets dapple my back as I realize what I've done. I may have prematurely signed my death warrant to evade pleasuring him.

His pursed lips spew water from them. "Maybe I didn't catch that right, woman. Did you…did you just say you done kill't yet another bastard?"

Vomitus churning over rust stains only inches from my face, a raging abuser triggered and poised is hovering inches above. Little moments like these remind me of what I'm reduced to, like ant stings while watching dreams devoured in a housefire.

"You got maybe three seconds, Meyrick."

"There's another man…another body. I didn't—I'm not the one, Leroy. I promise you this isn't me doing this."

"Where…Meyrick?"

"The coop. Just behind the coop."

A harrow plow through earth, his hot fingers work their way up the back of my scalp, parting my hair between them. A clenched fist secures me painfully within his grasp. "You're about to learn today."

I fill my lungs with the sour scent of bile, anticipating his malevolent actions. I don't feel my face slap the water, not initially. I'm painfully pinned between his steadfast grip and the inside of the bowl as his force compresses my cheeks and forehead into the concave porcelain under the water. So agonizing is the ordeal that I pray to lose consciousness, yet I keep my breath locked tight.

I'm limp. I'm cognizant of the cool, wet flooring under either flaccid hand…it will need tending to promptly if he gives me back my breath. Limp. Though, the boiling angst in my chest has warm urine pooling pathetically beneath me, yet another mess.

I'm nearing the threshold. Discreetly rebelling against my body's will to live won't be an option much longer. I've witnessed a cat grow uninterested of toying with a lifeless baby hare—exhausted by the cat's cruel antics, the hare merely wandered away once the cat did. Am I the hare? Is he the cat?

The urge to move, to inhale and breathe is too strong. I gently press against his grip. The action instantly has him bearing down his full weight. I feel as though my cheekbones may crush beneath him before I drown.

I open my mouth, ready to take in my ending.

My head hits the wall, perhaps the floor, with a blackening force as I'm flung backwards, but the breath

I draw is the sweetest. The sensation of tiny prickling pins all about my face and body has me spasming with each inhalation and I'm unsure if I'm completely conscious or somewhere in between. I only know I'm breathing.

On my side, face in a puddle on the floor, his feet come into view. *I want to live.* Why do roaches and rodents scamper only to squalor, they long to exist. Perhaps this violent tribulation is actually a revelation smeared in vomit and doused in toilet water.

"Meyrick."

"Please," I choke out. "Please don't kill me."

Something about his chuckle is off. Disingenuous. He squats to me, naked and dripping. My gaze is all that moves as we connect, and in this moment there's a fraction of something I can relate to. There's smidgeon of what might be guilt in his expression—a bit of a human.

Trembling, I reach slowly for his foot and rest my hand atop it. A silent plea for mercy.

"Clean…you get this shit cleaned up," he mutters. "Then we'll talk about your shenanigans."

There isn't a melody that can rival the grandeur of his feet slapping the floor as he leaves me. I'm alive.

For the next several seconds I'm stationary—stuck to the floor under a quilt of impassiveness. When I do move, finally, it is methodical…as if I'm a marionette being lifted from a lifeless state.

Strawberry bruising embellishes my cheeks and forehead when I gander my reflection. They'll be an ugly purple tomorrow and a hideous yellow-green next week if I'm still upright. They'll fade. They always do. Now, however, I'm faced with the peculiar inkling of longing for more than that…more than fading. I long to outlive my bruises, and that's abnormal as I stare at the injured woman before me, drenched and bloodshot.

My assessment is disrupted as polite taps on the thin glass above the tub have my gaze diverting to the small, rectangular window and I'm unsurprised to see a raven perched on a nearby branch and peering inside. I allow the cordial corvid all but two seconds of my time. Allotting anything additional to illusions seems even more insane than the hallucination itself. I return to my reflection, and it continues tapping about on the glass, until it doesn't…and it's gone.

There was a world beyond the community. There must be a world, or at the very least some safe harbor, beyond this wretched and cruel place. Be it with the company of the murderous duo or all alone, I must escape. I must scamper, even if it's to squalor.

***

I could open my belly and pull and cut things away and it might be less agonizing than the idea of Kaleb being cut from me forever. He shook. To see him shiver and the light extinguished from his eyes as they carried him away was torturous.

The night comes with the sounds of heavy boots and stern voices from the floor below the bedroom. The sky outside the window darkens and speckles with stars before Jennet finally opens the bedroom door looking peaked and poorly.

"Jennet!" The appropriate action might be to embrace her. So livid am I with the situation that I long to slap her, so I remain still instead and watch her from across the room.

"Meyrick. Oh Meyrick, it was awful."

"What! What was awful? Tell me he hasn't faced the reeds—"

"No," she interjects. "Tomorrow. When the sun rises." Palm to her chest, she chokes on her words. "He'll be led to the Church courtyard."

"How many members will hold reeds?"

Tears stream as her face collapses in emotion.

"How many, Jennet!"

"All of them!" she screeches.

I sit on the bed behind me, bewildered by the circumstances. The ticking clock is quick to remind me that time is of the essence. "What time, tomorrow?"

"At dawn's light, Meyrick."

"Okay. I haven't much time then." I stand and move for the window.

"Time for what?" she asks.

"To save him…I'm going to save him."

"How would you propose to do that?" A baritone voice, stern and steady, barrels through the room. I turn to see Kaleb's father in the doorway.

"Sir?"

"Go on." He moves into the room.

"I haven't time for discussion. I must go to my husband."

His arms uncross. "You were just telling me, Meyrick, of how you intend to save my dear son."

"Perhaps…perhaps you misheard me—"

My wrist is snatched up in his grasp. "Do not speak lies under my roof, girl."

I yank away rebelliously. "What then? Go on, fetch the Community Leadership. I'll face the reeds alongside him tomorrow."

His chin raises as if he's summing me up the way

men do one another. "You have a certain strength to you, Meyrick. So do enlighten me as to how you plan to save Kaleb from his sentence. You are but a girl—"

"I am a woman, strong, and more than capable of taking my husband from the shaking clutches of this pathetic place." I step to him.

His chuckle isn't condescending. I can almost taste a hint of relief in the air. "What will you need?"

"I beg your pardon?" I abrasively respond.

"What will you need to take my child safely from here?"

"I need nothing more than you to move out of my way."

"Meyrick," he barks as I attempt to maneuver around him. "If your agenda is to storm the Church dramatically before the two of you disappear into the night, I assure you, you will fail."

"And I assure you I will not. There is nothing in this world or the next that will keep me from the lifetime I was promised with him. I will collect him. I will save him."

"I believe you." His tone is softer. "Let me help you."

Kaleb's mother appears from the hallway shadows, her face lit with hope. "We'll both help you."

My anger melts like warm butter. "Okay. We haven't much time and we can't implicate this household." Shoulders back, head high, I assert some form of authority over my husband's wellbeing and it is simultaneously liberating and horrifying.

"Henry," Jennet stammers, catching the room's attention. He isn't departing for two more days, but with a decent payout he might be persuaded to leave

earlier."

"We've given him all we have for the three of us to leave as scheduled."

"What?" Kaleb's father interrupts.

"Are you truly surprised that the young people of this oppressive society might long for something more? Tell me you're not that delusional, sir."

"I won't go," Jennet blurts. "I'll stay behind. The paid portion should more than cover the two of you and an early departure. Perhaps, Father, you might contribute something more—

"Oh!" I'm beneath a frigid downpour. The hot water has subsided and instantly the steamy shower I was reminiscing under has become almost intolerable.

Dried and dressed I once again examine my facial wounds, ballooning and discolored, prior to facing whatever the remainder of the day offers.

There's a world outside this bathroom door, and although I face it daily, today I'm doing so with a yearning for preservation.

There's relief in finding Leroy's truck is gone.

"Emily," Anna's voice whispers in the kitchen.

"Anna!" My palm presses to my pelting heart. "You scared me half to death."

"Good." She strolls from the corner near the stove. "Many more are coming. You know this, yes?"

"Anna, why are you in the house? He could be back anytime—"

"We need to be done with Leroy. Your pretty face is pretty no more. We will kill him when the time is perfect."

"Anna. We need to leave this place. You, me, and Q. We need to leave while—"

Her slender index finger presses gently to my moving and aching lips. "Sshhh. This is the home. We must protect it, sweet Emily."

"The home? Protect it how?"

"Killing all who come here like, how do you say…moths to the fire, until the time has come for Leroy's suffering."

Her confident proclamation has me shaking my head in objection. "No, Anna. That's insane. No more killing. We can't. We have to leave."

"Go where, Emily? So stupid." She turns angrily from me. "You don't see them, but they watch from the trees like coyotes. Their eyes can't glow when they're as dark as the night around them, but they are there, and they are waiting."

Her words are senseless, yet I'm growing perplexed. "Who? Who is waiting in the trees, Anna?"

"Those who seek revenge. Those who seek to stomp us out like we are the vermin."

"Anna, they seek revenge for the men we've buried in shallow graves around this home. A home that is not ours."

"You know nothing!" The anger in her eyes matches that in her voice.

"Then tell me what it is I do not know, Anna."

"Revenge is coming for him. When he is gone, revenge comes no more."

"Then let us leave this place—"

"To where, you fool? When Leroy is gone and the eyes in the trees are closed for good, we will begin our new life in our own nest. Do you not understand this, Emily?"

"You would slay this monster and then take his

den?" I enquire scornfully.

"You are here, yes? This monster is feeding you and keeping you warm. You sleep next to him each night while talking of your husband…letting him hurt you and for why?"

"Anna—"

"Take what you can while you can. Take the home for our own. Take his life and then his farm. When he is gone the coyotes no longer prowl in the trees. If they do, we will plant them perfectly all next to the pretty flowers in your little garden. We will kill them, Meyrick. All of them."

She exits prior to further debate. Thoughts of devilish beings, upright coyotes with blackened eyes and pink-stained grins, tucked in the trees like reserved nightmares, have me reeling within. If there's the slightest hint of realism to her cautioning, then this trickling siege could flood a torrent of wrath at any time. The unremitting aching in my face reminds me such a threat exists in a singular version within the bastard, Leroy. What validity might there be in her argument to end him? There's no moral opposition to the idea of taking Leroy's life. The idea has often slipped into the realm of fantasy. How, is the question.

Any frail hand might successfully plunge a reasonably sharpened blade into the chest of an incapacitated drunk. His demise could come swiftly. To be truthful, I've often longed for his sorrow. My heart has yearned to taste his grief and delight in his distress the way he has in mine. Perhaps monsters beget monsters or the making of such. My grisly intentions have never fruited to anything more than intentions. Many nights I've stood over him with ill objectives twisting my brain's natural course. Something halted me. Understanding that the world's hatred of me is a bit more intense than his is seemed to loosen my grip round the knife…hammer…or jug of kerosene. I'd always tuck those things away and slip back under the bedding with him. Some nights I'd even reach for his sleeping hand and imagine it to be Kaleb's—warm and loving. Some mornings when he'd reach for me, I'd seal my eyelids and paint visions of Kaleb along the backs of them as Leroy barreled into me like a soiled object. Grunts and aggression always wash those images of Kaleb away and I'm left looking for faces.

A lax breeze whistles through the screen door. Soft and soothing and opposite the sharp bite of Anna's disposition. Her words have my mind mingling senseless thoughts with blistered emotion.

Through the door and down the steps I stumble—in pursuit of clarification. Nearly to the barn, passion enters my ears. Giggling and short, shrill shouts urge me to pause and progress easily.

My fingertips and left ear press to the barnwood, anxious for answers. Spoken words are unrecognizable, yet tantalizingly beautiful from the other side. Lovemaking banter seems identifiable in any language.

It's useless to deny that it is envy accelerating my heartrate. The idea of their entanglement, skin dappled in perspiration, eyes bright with exhilaration as their bodies meet as one, has my fingers digging into the timber. Navigating my emotion is proving difficult. Am I aching for my lost lover? Perhaps I'm angered by their ability to take pleasure in what I cannot? Or do I long for them? For her?

"Emily!" Anna's friendly and excited voice calls to

me. "Open the door. Come to us."

I look about frantically, wondering how I've been exposed as I step softly backwards from the barn.

"Don't leave, my beauty. Open," she calls once more.

I'm moving for the door and pulling it open before my mind can process what I'm doing. As my eyes adjust from the bright outdoors, they ingest the splendor before me. My body ignites in excitement as I witness them in the hay, unclothed and rolling about carelessly. They roll softly, chuckling, and halt with Q atop of her…inside of her. His palms flat to the earth on either side of her face, he braces himself above her as he thrusts passionately into her…and yet her gaze is transfixed on mine.

"Only watching, Emily?" she asks as her finger traces along his muscular back.

"This…this is private. I should go—"

"Stay," she interjects.

So impacted am I by what I am witnessing that I feel my core on the verge of eruption. She rolls him over, her shadow-drowned hair shimmering in the scattered rays wriggling through the barn walls and roof above. He repeats the action and is on top once more…rolling.

Just as I'm quivering, nearly convulsing, my gaze rests on two feather-cloaked beings wrestling about the hay and dirt below me—squabbling ravens.

"No!" My hands cover my eyes. "This isn't real. You're not….you're not—"

"Emily!" Her hand rests upon my shoulder as I open my eyes to Anna, as taken aback as she is clothed.

"What?" I stammer.

"Are you okay? Acting so strangely."

"This makes no sense. Your clothes…and, and Q?"

She glances over her garments and back at me. "My clothes? They are clean, yes? And Q is napping in the sun."

"I…we were just…" my words trail as I look upon bodiless hay.

"You need sleep, Emily. The brain has many enemies. Sleep is not one of them. Go to rest, now. This evening we have much for discussion. Much for planning. You need sleep."

15.

"The west end. Remember, if you are captured, Henry's name cannot be uttered. Repeat mine one-million times but Henry's can't leave your mouth, child. This is still his home," Kaleb's father exclaims—anticipation mounting in his voice. The way he breathes feverishly and glances about like a fleeing animal while peering from the window only enhances my anxiety.

"They're watching the home now, Meyrick," he continues. "Yet, I'm certain they'd never expect an attempted rescue."

"It won't be attempted," I mutter, snaring the room's attention. "I will be successful."

"Listen to my words, child. Kaleb is secured, yet only Bartholomew watches over him—"

"Have you forgotten I am well versed in the proceedings, my dear father-in-law? I too sat under their watchful eye, tearful and waiting for daylight and their verdict."

Through the aged glass I peer toward the Church once more while filling my chest with stale air and assurance. "It is time. The sun rises in less than an hour. Let me go to the shadows of the forest."

For but a brief moment I can hear their hearts beating and their tears screaming as they look to me for resolution. I realize the heart racing is my own. The screaming tears are silent farewells. Regardless the outcome, I'll never stand with these individuals again.

"Oh, Meyrick," Jennet rushes to me, embracing me. "Please know I love you."

Her arms are heavy around my neck—suffocation.

"Yes. And I you."

We decouple as I collect my satchel, and all the courage I can muster. "I wish you all the best life. Think of us often. Know we are happy."

Silence is agonizing but necessary as I take the first step toward the backdoor. I disregard their faces as I move past and into the night. The trees reach for me, welcome me with their slender branch fingers. Under a blanket of singing and screeching nightly things, I dart along worn trails and toward the Church.

The Church boasts the only visible light, a singular lamp on the lower level shining from inside. Mr. McCormick is correct in stating the Community would never suspect an attempted rescue. No one could ever be so brazen and sinful.

Like the McCormick home, the Church is nestled quite close to the tree line of the forest. I peer toward the door of the building, steadying my breath as I collect my wits.

My feet are boulders, solid and drumming as I race toward the Church, up the stairs, and to the door. My quivering hand rests atop the doorknob. It whines as I turn it and I'm unsurprised to find it unlocked. The Church is never locked.

A hint of lavender and pine enters my nose. The front room is silent and illuminated by a soft glow. My initial caution dampens as I move from the parlor and follow the light.

Sobs. Soft sobs and prayers lead me to him. From the doorway I look upon my beautiful Kaleb, kneeling next to Bartholomew, hands clasped atop a worn pew.

He shakes still—Bartholomew's arm is draped about his shoulder for comfort.

I inhale, retrieving the blade from my satchel. He is not theirs.

"Let us go now, Kaleb." My stern words turn their faces. Kaleb's eyes are swollen nearly shut as I enter the room.

"Meyrick," Bartholomew mutters. "Leave us now, and this will never be mentioned. You have my word."

Securing my footing and my grip on the blade's handle, I glare down on the Community elder. "Do you see even a dash of honesty in me, Bartholomew?"

He nods aggressively. "Yes, child. I see you are good and favorable in the light of—"

"Then believe me when I say I will kill you if you attempt to keep me from taking my husband from this place."

His eyes widen in disbelief. His lips move—wordless.

"Meyrick, what is…I don't understand. What are you doing?" Kaleb cries out.

"Kaleb, stand. We are leaving, now."

He shakes his head, his gaze toward the floor. "I can't…I don't understand…"

"Look at me!" My shouting snaps their faces forward. "You'll have the remainder of your life to fuss and carry on about this incident but right now…Kaleb, right now I need you to collect your wits, to be a man, and pull yourself together, because if you can't then I can't help you."

"H…help me?"

"Yes. I'm here to save you. So, stand and let us go, binds and all."

The variation in his expression is instantaneous. His eyes rejuvenate with hope. "Okay…yes, okay."

"You risk your eternal—"

"Silence, Bartholomew!" I interrupt. "Hear me well, old man. There are several fellows just outside these doors. They stand ready to strike and burn this Church to ash with you inside if you so much as peek out that damned door once we've departed."

He appears emotionally vacant as he ingests my warning and merely nods.

"Now, Kaleb!"

Stumbling as he stands, Kaleb manages to his feet and hobbles to me with hands bound before him. I guide him down the hallway and out the door to the open arms of the night. "The west end."

"Meyrick, how?"

"Be silent, Kaleb. Your only job is to remain alive." I tote him behind me like a child. The scratching, prodding branches soon open to a gorgeous sight...Henry's baby-blue flatbed.

"On the dot, Meyrick!" he proclaims from the driver's side window, slapping his hand aside the outside of the door.

"Climb aboard, Kaleb." I assist him and scurry up after as the vehicle spurts and moves and grumbles away from all we know.

"You did this, Meyrick," Kaleb gasps.

"Indeed," I reply, mildly dazed. "It appears I have."

"Where is Jennet?"

16.

"Jennet." I awake to a dim-lit room. I feel Kaleb fading from me. Only moments prior I sat next to him and now he's leaving me like moonlight at dawn. His scent, his words, and the way we blend beautifully into one another are the greatest gifts and they're vaporizing.

"No. Put me back," I whimper into my hands as I role to me side.

I was never one to cast a curious glance on the young men of my community. Like marked saplings, I understood exactly what each would mature to be. Each one boasting a voice louder than his peers. Each one vowing to cast aside any and all who disagree in the slightest with the stanch regulation suffocating my people—an orchard of toxicity.

Kaleb was different. I first felt comfortable breathing, and then talking freely in his presence. Not only did he listen but his eyes ingested my ideas. I spoke entire sentences without interruption or witnessing his expression warp in condemnation. He heard my words and I know in my heart they were precious to him. He was precious to me.

Leroy is my plague. He takes from me all that I love and leaves me at his mercy, begging to remain breathing, impoverished, and in his bed.

Who am I to assume Anna is eccentric or impractical? I am in no position to cast judgment on the psychosocial well-being of others. Perhaps her idea of slaying Leroy is not insane—I've envisioned it countless times.

I do know, however, that the idea of staying in this

home with my destructor any longer *is* insane. The gradual depletion…slow-burn of an ending, is no more. He grasps at chunks of my existence now and flings them to a void. I will go to Anna and I will discuss her plans with her, and I will do so with an open mind.

Crying hurts. Engorged lips—split and seeping, and bloated blackening eyes leave little leeway for physical emotion. A bag of frozen carrots from the freezer feels dreadful when initially applied to the affected areas.

A glance in the bathroom mirror births the idea that my horrendous appearance might nudge Leroy to complete the deed of ending me. I'm quite certain I'm breathing still only due to the fact he fancies my physical attributes.

A wailing stuns me. Haunting cries from outdoors have me rushing through the home to the front door, dreading what I might encounter.

A man, twenties or thirties and unkempt, strolls the yard distraughtly while calling out to someone. His gaze wanders the scene, high and low, as if whom he seeks is tucked in trees or blades of grass.

His voice is robed in agony, it echoes heavy on his cries as they carry across the lawn. I want to help him. I want to comfort him.

"Hello? You there!" We connect as I descend the steps.

"Monstre!" he yells, his face twisting in disgust as he looks on me.

"I beg your…*etes-vous Francais…Canadien? As-tu besoin d'aide?*" I ask as I stand cautiously at a distance.

His quivering grimace ensures me the likelihood of casual conversation is miniscule. Studying his face gives me nothing. This man is as foreign to me as the shores of Asia. Yet, his eyes pierce me. They harbor an identifiable hatred. Where is it stemming from? Where did he come from?

A hurting heart is a sponge drenched in hatred, multiplying like the worst bacteria—soggy and seeping the deadliest consequences. Fear is outweighed by curiosity. I remain affixed in place, studying the odd creature as he studies me.

Before I can enquire further details, the hardened lines of his face soften. The anger vacates his eyes, and he plummets to the ground as limply as a soggy sheet from the clothesline. Left standing behind him is a troublesome visual. Anna gawks downward momentarily. Blood glides like silk from the slender butcher knife in her hand. She nonchalantly examines the fingernails of her other.

"Ann…Anna?"

"You see, my love? So easy to remove," she exclaims with a casual grin.

My fingers shake as I bring my hands to cover my mouth. The slightest touch of my lips is electric pain. "Why?" I whisper into my palms.

"Every time is this fucking conversation. How do you say…delicate? So delicate, Emily!" She steps over the man as if he's a mild inconvenience, a log, or piece of garbage. Walking toward me, she shakes the blade free of excess blood. "All of them! Every one of them."

"Who…who is he, Anna? I don't know this man or who he was—"

Boisterous laughter fills the air. It cracks like thunder over the trees and yard as she throws her head back maniacally. "So stupid! You want to know each enemy? Seriously?"

Her laughter quells as she looks to me. Even now in her most heinous state, I find her entrancing. Her locks tossed messily by the breeze. Her eyes play peekaboo behind them…just above her playful grin—the grin of a mischievous murderess. "Emily, waste no tears on those who wish to make you cry." Her soft lips press to my cheek as gently as a dandelion.

"Anna—"

"Now, Emily, drag this bastard back to the trees he crawled from. Much planning, my love. So much planning."

The warmth has yet to leave his hands as I pull on them, inching him toward the tree line. His eyes half-pried, expose only the sliver of white as his head bounces unsupported over the gravel. He was here only moments ago and now he's being tossed away like chicken scraps. The senseless loss of life angers me and saddles me with additional questions. As if I've a jar for inquiries and it's to the brim.

I tuck him away amongst foliage and remorse—a grave unsuitable for a sparrow, let alone a stranger. His face bears the morning's markings, scratches and debris from our unfortunate encounter, but nothing substantial to suggest this man is of a hardened life. He's soft, folded up and left to fall from the pages of history as if he were never scribbled there. This moment has me hating myself.

The water isn't hot enough to scorch the blood from my hands. The kitchen sink reeks of a bloody metallic scent that permeates the air and coats the inside of my mouth.

Humans do such enchantingly magnificent things. We construct tall buildings, write hypnotic melodies and literature and yet…looking to the collection of fly corpses spotting the windowpane, I'm reminded life is only as imperishable as we pretend it to be. We're as fragile as flies.

Outside once more, I roam the yard, glancing about curiously for any additional marauders or the man's vehicle. I find nothing. His face, the pain waving through his expression, won't leave my thoughts. He was somebody's son…somebody's friend or lover…he was somebody. *He was somebody* and he was here for answers to questions I'm clueless to. And now he is dead.

The hours fade, yet the man's words, his voice, will not. Leroy arrives as the sun settles in on the west end of the sky. This is anything but atypical except he doesn't storm through the door, cursing and making demands. He walks somberly up the steps, head down, brow creased as he steps into the home. He avoids looking at me initially, and when he does it's only momentarily. I feel I was right to be concerned, he may dispose of me now that I'm broken and hideous—scarred and unusable.

"Meyrick—" he mutters.

"If you're to kill me, do me the decency of referring to me by my preferred name, Leroy. Emily." I assume my hasty interruption will ignite anger, but he only looks toward the floor, ballcap in his hands.

"Em…well, hell then…Emily, I done went too far, woman." He nods his head confidently, as if reassuring his words to be accurate. "You're the woman of the house. You got…you got duties just like I do. And you can't do them duties if you's all busted all to hell. You's just as busted up as me, and that ain't right. So…so I give you my word, woman, what happened this morning won't happen again."

"Leroy," I mutter. "Leroy, I know it's been difficult. I appreciate your kind gesture."

He only nods.

"May I, if you don't mind…I'm not feeling well, may I lie down before preparing supper?"

To my surprise, again, he nods.

***

The word freedom sounds gorgeous enough. Yet taken from a book or song, freedom has no context…no structure. Freedom is a brisk, northern wind, or the bliss, seconds after ingesting the richest poem. Freedom is a sip of cool water, but it is not what is shouted sternly in the history books. I fear we would perish…starve and whittle if we were served a slice of what we claim to crave. We're most secure behind locked doors and under rule of government. And yet, as I'm jostled about in the dark, stars high above me, Kaleb at my side, I am secure in the knowledge that I am free of my father. I will die before his hand rests upon my shoulder…before his words enter my ears again.

"Meyrick," Kaleb sighs, his head in my lap as we ride down the road in the back of the truck—far from the community and into the unknown.

"Yes."

"Who are you?"

Assuming he's referring to my fiendish actions during the rescue, I merely chuckle.

"I'm serious," he repeats, propping himself up. "You can be anyone you want now. Who do you want to be?"

The comment swirls about in my brain until it's senseless as abstract watercolor. "I've always loved me, Kaleb. I love being me. I love being...wait...Emily," I mutter.

"Emily?"

"Yes. Emily McCormick."

He grins. "I love it."

"What will we call you?"

Burying his face in my lap, he chuckles. "Um, Herbert...or Cletus..."

"Cletus?" I stammer as he looks up to me, grinning as the air and dust whisk around us from over the truck sides.

"I'm not serious. I'm no good with picking names, never had much need to be."

The stars swim in his eyes as our gazes lock. "Until now, Mr. McCormick," I say slyly, maneuvering his hand upon my belly as I witness his expression twist and twitch. "Meyrick...are you...are you with child?" He sits up, eyes wide as he attempts to conceal his smile.

"I know no Meyrick, Kaleb...but Emily...Emily McCormick is indeed blessed with your daughter or son in her belly—"

"I'm to be a father?" he shouts, slapping his forehead.

"Yes, the best father."

There is no controlling his emotion. It takes his words and floods his face.

"I love..."

"I know you do. I love you too. I know this will be difficult, but we'll make it work. I feel it in my bones that we'll make this work, Kaleb. You are my life.

You're why I'm breathing."

I take his hand while pounding the glass of the rear-window, motioning Henry to stop. As he comes to a halt, dust and dreams thick all around us, I leap from the side.

"Henry!" I exclaim through the driver-side window, filling the cab which holds Henry and two others.

"That is my name. This has been established."

"Give me two minutes."

Kaleb is motioned to join me as we stand stationary in the dark, center of the road. "Don't you see, my love?" I take his hands, they tremble in my grasp. The moon dances in the tiny streams leaving his eyes.

"I see you."

"And I see you. And this world." I squeeze firmly. "What else is there? Look to the stars, Kaleb. They're countless. What else do we need? We're rich! I'm the richest woman alive!"

"Hey!"

My gaze settles to a blanket of gray clouds above me—starless.

"Hey now!" Leroy's voice is a hot-match head pressed to flesh. "Woman."

I look to Leroy, half-bent with hand extended as if he's approaching an irritated bovine at large. "You done got any sense you had left knocked plum out of you." He inches closer. "Talkin' at yourself in the damn driveway—"

I look about the area, startled yet unsurprised to be far from my husband and instead in front of this man. Kaleb's face and voice pulls away painfully like cloth from a healing wound.

"You didn't have to kill him, Leroy." The words

move from me as casually as rushing water. "He was innocent. He was good. You didn't have to—"

"He made a choice, Meyrick…Emily," he chuckles.

"A choice?" My voice cracks as I step forward—the rocks in the drive, digging into my feet. "What choice? The only choice was coming here, and given the choice we would have left—"

"Then leave!" he rages toward me, sending me stumbling back. "Go. There's the goddamned road. I ain't gonna stop ya. Not now, not never."

I pace my breath as he stops several feet in front of me. "I'm sorry, Leroy."

"You'll never leave…say it."

"Leroy—"

"Say it!"

"I am yours."

The ashen atmosphere wraps us like a suffocating quilt of misery as we face one another.

"Go on then…take you another one of them long, hot baths you enjoy so much. Soak it up and all that." He tosses his hand up before walking away.

I'm left to wonder what choice my husband was left to make, how he died, and where his final resting place might be.

The bath I draw isn't only hot, it's all but unbearable as I slink in up to my chin. There's a part of me that longs for some wild commotion from the sitting room to interrupt my relaxation. A part of me that longs for Anna to rush through the door of the home with her disarming grin and deadly blade and be done with Leroy. I do crave his demise, and yet it horrifies me simultaneously. Like a battered, chewed up lamb, anxious at the thought of lacking the company of her coyote to lie down with of an evening, there's an uneasy feeling circulating the idea of Leroy's death that I can't quite categorize. It sickens me that it exists within my psychology, yet it is there.

The heat centers me. As I gently place a dampened washcloth atop my face, I hear knocking from either of the home's entries—which one, I am unsure. *Could it be Anna with her blade?* I sit forward and am somewhat relieved to hear an unrecognizable baritone voice when Leroy opens the door. The conversation is muffled, but the man speaking sounds American.

My heart races with curiosity. I scurry from the tub. Wrapped and dripping, I tiptoe to the door.

"He specifically mentioned coming here," the man's voice says.

"I done said I ain't seen him. I'd tell you—"

"I heard you, Leroy. Those are words. Words are worthless from a man like you."

The man's comment leaves my mouth agape. He must be a man of power, extremely dangerous, or both, to comfortably speak to Leroy in such a way. Silence takes the home. I stand, fearful to inhale, that my breath might be heard.

"He was a hand. He left. That's what they do. Ain't nothin' to get your feathers ruffled over."

"That boy is in my favor, Leroy."

"That don't explain why the fuck he'd a come traipsin' round here—"

"You know goddamned good and well why he would have come here, you barbaric mongrel! If he is here, if you're lying about his whereabouts…I'll do things to you that'd make a butcher gag, and while you're still breathing."

I hear the screen-door slam. The man leaves with no rebuttal from Leroy and I am left with a head of questions, shivering under steaming-red skin. I retreat to the water once more. Just as I slip in, Leroy enters.

"Hey," he shouts, peering through the doorway—grasping the doorknob.

"Yes, Leroy?"

"You ain't seen another fella round here today…um, a white fella, pretty boy who looks like he ain't never worked a field in his life?"

I shake my head no.

"You sure bout that?"

"I'm sure, Leroy."

"Good. If you do see a stupid bastard fittin' that description, you be sure send his ass on up the road."

"Who…who was he, Leroy?"

He stares at me from the doorway for a moment. "Just a hand. But this ol' boy wasn't the likes of Ricardo's heathens. He's better suited at books and what not than a real man's work. But that fucker, Henson, took to him a year or so back and I imagine he'll be hard at it until he finds his dumb ass."

"Why?"

"What?" he snaps angrily. "I got no clue why folks take a liking to their hands. Maybe he reminds him of his son, maybe he likes it in the tailpipe—"

"Why would he come here?" I interject, sitting up.

He chuckles. "No idea. Seems to me plenty of trash blown in lately." He steps into the bathroom. "You said, was."

"I beg your pard—"

"You asked who he *was*, not is." He peers down, examining every detail of my reaction.

"I meant nothing by it, Leroy. I'm tired…I've not seen the man."

Still peering, he nods prior to exiting.

***

"Anna!" I call as I enter the barn. When I need her company or counsel, she is nowhere to be found, but when a stranger is lurking about, she appears readily with blade in hand.

"Anna, I need you now!"

The last of the light is slipping from the barn as my eyes struggle to adjust and find my assassin companion. "Anna, please, if you're here…it must be tonight."

A sultry silhouette appears from the opposing side of the barn. "Emily. Please, it is too much noise for such a peaceful setting. Keep your voice soft."

"What?" Appalled, I move toward her. "Don't…just stop. You have me in the worst bind. You've acquired yet another body that I must dispose of and if Leroy finds the man before he's in the ground, he'll put me there as well."

Anna remains guarded, tucked within a collection of shadows. "Leave the dead man where he is, Emily," she says tenderly.

"What? Are you insane? I am under the same roof as a madman."

"Soon…all in time, my beautiful."

Nonchalant and monotone, her detached demeanor has me beginning to boil. "Soon? Soon what? Anna, soon I may be disposed of like the men you have murdered."

"No. Do not worry so. You know how this ends—"

"Stop saying that! I don't know how this will end.

Neither do you. I don't know you or your motives or if either of us will be upright and breathing in two days' time. Do not tell me I know the ending of anything when I'm clueless as to how this very hour might end!"

"Quiet! Now!" she snaps. "You have seen the sacrifices as you stand there watching." She's enraged as she emerges from the shadows.

"Sacrifices? Anna, we are surrounded—"

"What has changed? Nothing?"

"My life," I respond immediately as she approaches methodically. "My entire existence has been disrupted and entirely altered. You take life as casually as—"

"We protect! What else would you have us to do? Be weak? Stand and watch? Or stay limp and cry while he beats you? Takes you? What do you want us to do? How can we give you back your precious life?"

As I digest her words, sour and revolting, I find they're drenched in truth. If not for Anna and her mate, I'd be without companionship. I'd be without any sense of purpose. I'd be completely alone. "What am I to do? I don't know what to—"

"Nothing! You do nothing. You wait until it is time." She moves to me, taking my hand.

"I don't understand."

"And that is okay. All will be okay. I promise."

Warm and soothing, her hands cradle mine like an infant in a mother's arms. I should turn from her madness. I should shield my eyes and ears from it but I don't. I breathe her air and gaze her smile and set aside my gathering of concerns as if they're trivial. This moment, these little moments, leave me craving more—to be human and to do human things freely and happily.

"Anna—"

"Sshh…" Her fingers work the hair from my face and secure it behind my ear. "You are beautiful under this worry. You are beautiful under these bruises." She brings my hand to her lips for a sisterly kiss. "And I promise, my sweet Emily, you will be beautiful when it is done. It will all soon be done."

Nothing about this equation makes sense, yet I find I'm longing to trust this plan I'm clueless to and let her guide me blindly. "Okay."

***

The night is lonely and still. Lying motionless on my side, listening to Leroy snore drunkenly, I find myself plastered with too many fragments of emotions to classify my current state of mind. The timing of his monstrous inspirations, constant and consuming, drowned my thoughts and I drift…

"Meyrick! Wake up!"

I'm being shaken gently from my shoulders.

"Emily. That will take some getting used to."

I open my eyes to daylight choked in fog and tall birch, a grinning Kaleb and a stalled truck on a lonely road bearing an uncanny resemblance to the one from the previous evening. "Kaleb, what are you—"

"We're in America, my wife! We made it to America!" The excitement in his voice and on his face—teaming in his eyes, is enough to have me grinning sleepily and propping myself up in the bed of the truck.

"We're in America right now, you say?"

"That's right," Henry confirms from behind me.

"Do you smell that?" Kaleb asks as he glances about the gray-covered scene. "Do you smell our

freedom?"

"I only smell my need for a bath," I reply as I stand, taking his hand. "Where we're headed...is it as beautiful, Henry?"

"It is beautiful," he replies, resting his elbows on the truck-bed side. "Freedom comes with a bounty of work. The two of you will be starting anew and that means callouses and sunburnt skin." He smirks empathetically. "You'll have a roof and full bellies—"

"Freedom is an illusion, my friend," I respond confidently. "We're only here for the opportunities we'd be denied back home. We're willing to dirty our hands...or bloody them."

"That's the spirit, then." Henry slaps the truck hood before leaving to the trees.

"When will we arrive, Kaleb?"

"Today...tonight." Kaleb continues glancing over the area.

There isn't much variation from where we grew up, yet he looks at it as if it's entirely unique to him. Miles of trees cloaked in blankets of fog—calls of countless birds whistling through branches. I could walk from this road and into the trees in any direction and it might look remarkably similar to my childhood backyard. And still, I've never been further from my childhood. I've never been safer. "We're the safest we've ever been, Kaleb."

Our gazes meet—his face is dewed by mist and illuminated with possibility. "What?"

"Now, in this second, roofless and without resources, we're the safest we've been in our entire lives—away from our community and our parents. We're safe."

I hear him swallow, over the swaying trees and rustling things, I hear the tension mount and tumble down his throat. "I've always felt safe with you, Meyrick...Em...Emily." He squeezes my hand. "You're the strongest human I know, ten-fold stronger than I. You've always made me feel protected. I feel...I feel safest with you."

His words are the purest. Our patriarchal community is saturated in a testosterone-toxicity that leaves little room for words such as these. I do not take them for granted. "Kaleb, I too feel safe with you. You are—"

"You saved me, Meyrick." He squares his feet to face me. There's an intensity creasing his brow, flaring his nostrils. "You did what was impossible. You took me from them. I would have...Bartholomew said I would have perished by the reeds. That was their intention. You stopped that."

"I opened a door and assisted my husband from his knees...left an elderly bastard to shiver. That isn't strength, Kaleb. You are everything to me."

"No. You're strong, Meyrick. You're stronger than me and I wouldn't be capable of any of this without you."

My husband; blind to his might, yet humble and kind. His eyes and stance are all but screaming for my embrace. As I press him into me, I admire how we physically fit into one another. "Kaleb, you needn't worry of doing any of this without me," I mutter into his shoulder. "If we remain cautious, yet ambitious with our futures, we will capture everything we set out after."

His arms are two broad limbs around me. I stand

motionless, breathing in the scent of exhaust and dust. One word wisps past my ear. "Potatoes?"

I chuckle as we decouple and take each other's hands. "Yes, my love. Potatoes."

17.

Strength. I once found it in various places. The most precarious scenes seemed to yield bits of courage from the nooks, and from those bits sprouted action. There are no bits in nooks here…none of strength anyhow.

Leroy has left for the fields. The smell of gingerroot and honey hangs heavy in the home. I'm preparing tea as I clean in the early morning hours. I've yet to visit the smallest of the barns. My guests will surely make me aware of their appetite once they're eager to quell it. Hanging the laundry will be completed last. I fear the morning air outside will be laced with a hint of death…his death.

Counters wiped and dusting done, I move to the bedroom to remove the sheets for washing. Something odd catches my attention. A picture on the floor glares up toward the ceiling. There are no pictures in this home—no framed memories. I approach the photograph as cautiously as a hornets' nest. Standing over them, looking down on the beautiful young couple staring back, I feel my breath snatched from my lungs as I recognize the man looking up at me to be the same man Anna buried the knife in—the same man I tossed to the ditch to rot.

I collect the photo in my trembling grasp for closer inspection. The two of them, grinning and embraced, could be faces from my community. Leroy must have drunkenly misplaced this last night. Thoughts dance in my head—theories crossing and mingling about but no real resolution—no true answers. And so I'll seek validation.

I race from the home and to the barns, calling for

Anna as I run. Photo in hand, I rush through the barndoor. "Anna!"

When neither of them is present, I head for the woodlands in hopes of finding them there. I'm winded by the time my ears catch the sound of their calls and laughter from the pond. I find them sitting on the bank and drying in the morning sun.

"Anna!" I call out as I approach. My boisterous arrival elicits a hefty scowl.

"Why are you so loud? So disturbing?" Anna asks as Q frowns at me from behind her.

"I have…" I clutch my knees, attempting to catch my breath. "I have something to show you."

"You show nothing by shouting."

I'm casually disregarded as her attention is returned to Q. The two talk tenderly, giggling like little girls in the back pew of a Sunday service.

"Anna, please," I ask softly. "Please look at this." I inch closer, displaying the photo inches from her face.

She sighs, her gaze settling on the faces a few seconds before shrugging. "What is this?"

"It's him," I stammer, shaking the picture.

"Who? I don't know who is him." Her tone and expression are riddled with frustration.

"Do you not see him? The man from the yard?"

Her expression hardens as she looks once more. "Oh." She turns her face from me, waving the photo away in dismissal. "I didn't see his face so much. You know?" She chuckles as she glances up once more. "I only saw him from the back," she adds with a smile.

"Anna, you killed him. You killed this man and I need to know who he was. I need to know who she is."

"Why? Why this is so important? Sit, relax. No more

questions and loud voice—"

"This is important, Anna! I need to know—"

"She is you, Emily!" Anna hisses as she arises from the bank. "That girl in the picture is you."

Her words are senseless and leave me shaking my head. "What? Don't be ridiculous, this woman looks nothing like me."

"She was you before you. You are the, how you say…replacement."

Validation.

The woman trembling in my grasp is young and beautiful, no older than I was when I came to this place. "Leroy took her," I mutter. "He took her from him, just as I was taken from Kaleb." The faces in the photo blur behind tears. My shared sorrow is shattered by Anna's unjustified snickering—it yanks my attention from the couple and to her crass grin. "You find this amusing? Humorous?"

"I find I don't care." Her reply comes slowly, the way people talk moments before drifting to sleep in the evening—sleepy eyes and smoky voice.

"Anna, what if this were you and Q? What if this nightmare happened to you?"

"This could never be possible. Never." She turns casually to help Q from the ground. He yawns as the two glance over the area dispassionately.

"I don't understand your mind, Anna. You're too cold. You're cruel."

Her sigh comes long—almost exaggerated, with her back to me. "Emily, your own mind you don't understand, yes? Maybe more time there."

"Anna—"

"I'm too cold…yet you come to me." She faces me.

"You need me. You asked for me."

"I asked for none of this, Anna," I snap, bewildered by her statement. "This man was likely looking for answers and he was murdered for it. I never asked for that."

I turn from them as a sickening sense of guilt festers within me.

"Where you are going, Emily?" she calls after me.

"To bury him! He deserves that at the very least."

Several meters from the drive I dig out a man-sized hole within the soft earth. Each spade-full of dirt I excavate has me detesting myself more. The final grave is anything but proper, but he won't be left to rot within weeds like carrion.

I pull him over rubble and twigs—his flesh spongy by time and rain. As he tumbles limply into the hole I've crafted him, mud and debris speckling his milky-white skin, I think of her. I wonder if she's breathing. I wonder if their story ends here or if his history will be muttered over lips of siblings or cousins. Will he be missed? Does she miss him still? Or does she rot in the ground somewhere in Idaho as well—buried away as dead as the dreams that brought her here.

I won't let him be erased. As the first spade-full of dirt falls about him, I make a silent promise to remember this man. He may be nameless to me but his grave will not go unbeautified. His pain will not be forgotten while I'm breathing.

Once he's completely covered, the mound of earth resembles nothing like the freshly dug graves from my community. The disrupted earth is as patchy as a mangy cat. There are twigs and vegetation and roots adorning the slightly raised hill. When I step on it to pack the earth tightly, I feel the softness of the man's body just below the surface. No proper grave, indeed…yet, I am no gravedigger.

The mound is covered in small rocks and a few flowers—nothing too conspicuous. When the task is complete and I am covered in muck—when the spade is aside and my hands bear sloughing blisters, I kneel to his grave. I once believed my heart to be pulverized. That cannot be. I ache. There's a physical ache within me as I clutch the stinging earth in my grasp. The pain in this man's eyes when I met his gaze was a pain all too familiar.

"Do you hear me now?" My voice sounds awkward and silly out loud. It has me glancing about for onlookers. "Do you hear my words?" I repeat, softly as a grandmother's whisper. The idea of God has often perplexed me. The thought of immortality or ghosts walking freely among us has more than once rolled my eyes. Yet, here I am, speaking to a dead man—seeking his counsel. "If you hear me, know I am truly sorry." My voice strains. "Know I would take your place in this shabby grave. I would take your place this very instant." A few tears make their way down my cheeks. "If there is more than this…if we are more than this…I hope you are with her now. I hope she's holding you and your pain is no more."

I release the dirt and dust my clothing as I rise. "You tell him I love him. You tell him I love him more each day and if he is there…if he is waiting, I'll be there soon."

***

There aren't pictures in books or those glossy taboo magazines that depict what we're witnessing. Faces of every color and age—a sea of diversity and scents surrounds us. We're waves within it. Henry is gone. He departed suddenly without farewell. Our elbows at any given time are inches from a stranger.

The barn we're in is thick with the scent of hay and musky odor. So loud are the assorted words of various languages that I'm deaf to what Kaleb is mumbling. Smoke dances in the glow of the lanterns hanging from the rafters just above our heads.

Without introduction, I am aware who is in charge. Men of a certain stature stroll the dusty crowd, observing us with a hunger in their eyes. Predacious as they appear, I remind myself they're my dream-keepers. They walk with confidence, scanning the crowds from under their straw and leather hats.

It's nearly two in the afternoon and the barn amplifies the swelter. Through the chaos, I notice individuals being selected—plucked from the masses by the gentlemen. As we're circulated toward the outer edges of the group of at least one hundred or more, a broad hand falls upon my husband's shoulder.

"Do you speak English?" a large gentleman asks. He's as big as a bear, towering over Kaleb. His head lacks hair and glistens in the lantern's light, and his mustache is a graying brown.

"I do, indeed," Kaleb replies chipperly. His response and kind smile appear unexpected, evidenced by the enquiring gentleman's expression.

"You from America or…like, Europe, or—"

"A small farming community in Alberta," Kaleb shouts back as we're nearly separated by people attempting to exit.

"Is that east or…whereabouts is that?" The man

grins while scratching his head. His smile resembles a decrepit wooden fence—panels broken or missing.

"Canada, my good sir."

"You say you can farm?"

"I surely can." Kaleb stands erect as if he's attempting to auction himself.

"Pay's once a month. Work is on the farm, not the field, but it's a man's work just the same. We got a hand-house we put our hands in. Ain't much, but it stays dry. There's a toilet, fridge, and bath."

Kaleb looks to me as if I'm to answer for him—his eyes are the widest I've ever seen them. "Are you offering me a job, sir?"

The mountain of a man peers down at my husband in confusion, hardening his expression. "That's why you're here, ain't it?"

"I accept," he utters. "Gladly."

"Kaleb!" I tug excitedly on the back of his shirt.

"Sir, this, I almost forgot about, Mey...Emily."

I'm gently maneuvered before the large gentleman. I could never imagine Goliath, regardless how well my mother painted his description. This man is the closest thing to a giant I've ever seen. He's enormous.

"How are you, sir?"

"I got no means for a woman's help," he sternly insists as the crowd gains additional faces from the open doors.

"I understand. I don't require much and I'm quite skilled at mending and washing. I'm learning to cook—
"

"I only got a need for hard labor." He sighs, eyeing Kaleb once more.

"I hope you find only the best, sir," Kaleb interjects.

"I'm sure my wife and I will, as well." Kaleb offers to shake the man's hand. As he does, the man grins once more.

"Oh. All right then. I'll take ya. Marriage is a beautiful thing. My wife'll likely enjoy having another lady-face around the place."

My husband's embrace comes instantly. "You hear that? We're employed!" he whispers excitedly into my ear.

"The name's Daniel. Daniel Squires."

"You won't be disappointed, sir. We'll work tirelessly," Kaleb proclaims.

"Let's get up out of here and get on the road. We got a good drive ahead of us and I aim to get the two of you fed and cleaned up. Work starts before the sun does."

"I could use a meal," Kaleb says as we follow Daniel out of the barn.

Food is the last thing on my mind. I only long to soak my cares away. I wish only for a bath...
***

I awaken soaking in cool, murky water. The tub is no place to drift and dream. I scrub away what is left of the morning wake and let it all retreat down the drain.

The knowledge I've gained will afford me nothing if it's prematurely disclosed. The picture has been tucked away so that I might fetch it when the time is appropriate.

The longing for details seems almost senseless. His story may not mirror mine yet the cruel reality is we both crawled to this land looking for something more— searching for scraps to piece together and claim as our own. What we found was a bounty of thirsty opportunists. I needn't see his tragedy written out to understand it. I've lived it as another character.

I was once convinced I lived among monsters—walled in by the trees. I once believed I could break from their twisted world if my feet could only carry me fast enough. Each smile I've gazed and acquaintance I've made since leaving my community has been that of a monster's. I find they're all warped, they're merely twisted by something else.

My beautiful Anna. It pains me to imagine what could have produced something so calloused. Behind her smile and those enchanting eyes is something quite insidious.

My world is a world of fiends. I fled a valley of them only to lie down with one of an evening and tend to two in secret. Where is my sanctuary?

My wet, loose hair falls freely about the back of my fresh gown as I fill the wash basket with damp clothing. At the clothesline, I hang the garments as the noon sun warms the top of my head. Socks and undergarments sway on the breeze. Monotony has its benefits. The numbing effects of repetitious tasks leave my mind blank and free to observe the raw simplicity around me.

As the second pin is placed on the largest of the white sheets, I'm stunned to find it slightly soiled—streaked with dirt and muck. The fabric isn't blemished with residual stains left after the wash. It boasts fresh dirt from an unknown source.

Instantly I inspect the basket to ensure the remainder of the clothing is unsoiled. As I return my attention to the half-pinned sheet, now draping untidily about the grass, I'm befuddled to see each other garment I've hung on the line bears mud and grime—it's all a mess.

"Im…impossible." The garments drying on the air are completely filthy. "I don't understand," I mumble as I reach for the sheet. As I do, I notice the filth and dirt on my hands and under my nails. Additional inspection shows I'm wearing a muck-covered gown, the same gown I wore to bury the gentleman rather than the fresh gown I exchanged it for. "No…I bathed. This isn't right—"

Commotion snares my attention. Complete chaos unfolds across the yard and through the weeds.

"They're eating him!" I spy a ghastly collection of winged grave-robbers rolling and fussing about through the vegetation surrounding the gravesite. I sprint toward the devilish assembly, waving my hands and attempting to scream—my voice has forsaken me.

As I near the scene I find myself hesitant to fully approach—fearful of what I will behold. The weeds provide just enough canopy that I catch only fragmented glimpses of the bickering ravens. They squabble and writhe within each other like a living, feathered fountain of oil bubbling from the core of the man I buried…only, it appears I never buried him. The slain man is ground-level and the excavated earth remains mounded behind the hole I dug.

"No. No, no, no!" I charge the birds, waving my hands to bat them away. They pay me no mind, as if I'm invisible to them. Their putrid feast continues—the awful noises of ripping flesh, shrills and caws enter my ears. The spade I used to dig the hole was never returned to the barn. I grab the handle and swing it wildly over the birds. I only wish to spook them, disperse them so I can finish what I thought I'd done previously.

True, they've long-time held my fascination and I've envied their strength and will. In this moment, however, I'm disgusted by the ravens and only wish they'd leave to the skies. "Go! Leave here, now!" I scream out as I continue waving the spade to no avail.

My gaze eventually falls on the stranger's face—what remains. Their beaks have torn and plucked away any identity remaining and what is left is hollow and horrifying.

The totality of the situation is overwhelming. "Go away! Leave here!" Squeezing my eyelids closed, I swing blindly. If there's any contact it's mild and the whispers of wings are heard lifting around me, as are the calls of protest as the birds take to the sky. "Leave!" I screech once more.

"Emily!" Anna's stern voice resounds just behind me.

Instantly, the blade is released as I turn to an astonished Anna and Q, witnessing the event from the driveway. "Anna! Anna, help me. Please help me."

I traipse from the mangled corpse, over and through the tall weeds to her. Monster or not, her touch is the only comfort left.

"Yes. Of course, my beauty. Help with what?" She grabs my shoulders, concern coursing in her eyes.

"I'd thought I buried him!" I shriek. "My mind told me I'd buried him!" I shake as I divulge. "I never did. I only left him to rot! To continue to rot. And they came! The ravens came. They were eating him! They ate him!"

"No!" Anna snaps sternly.

"Yes!" I nod insistently. "They were numerous and all about him! Pecking and devouring him—"

"This is untrue!" Anna snarls, shaking me. "This cannot be!"

"It is true! They tore his face to pieces—"

The sound her hand makes slapping my face is more saddling than the slap itself. "This is untrue, Emily!" She barks once more, before clutching my arm and whirling me to face the ransacked gravesite. "You see? No birds. Only flowers…rocks. You buried him."

My gaze falls on the shabby mound of earth, spotted with rocks and dandelions, and other various wildflowers. There is no eyeless, faceless corpse strewn sloppily aside a malformed hole in the ground. *I did bury him.* I look to my gown to find that it is the fresh one I'd changed into. "They were…I saw…" From across the yard I spot the laundry hanging on the line. There are no soiled items there—only white socks and undergarments and a poorly hung white sheet.

"Anna." I turn to her. "Anna, I don't understand. I saw them. I see things. My mind is broken."

She pulls me to her. "Tell me, have you ever met someone who is not broken?"

"Anna, I've gone insane."

"No, my beauty. Your mind is too tired to, how you say…cope, with the world you have left it in. You are so tired, Emily."

I observe the area once more—all of it. "I cannot afford to be tired. Not now. Now I must be vigilant, Anna. How am I to survive if I can't distinguish reality from illusion? I'm alone. My mind is my only asset and I feel it slipping violently!"

"You are not alone, my beauty. We are here. All will end how it is supposed to end. You must believe this."

I shake my head as I pull from her. "You say these

things so confidently, as if I'm to know the future or you have some divine knowledge. I only know that I live with a madman and my only ally in all the world delights in the act of bloodshed."

Anna gasps and chuckles simultaneously.

"And that my mind is unwell. My mind is sick."

"Oh! Here you are again, Emily." Anna's voice hardens once more. "Do you hear your words? Your stupid little words? If you take a healthy, fat little bird and leave her in a cage of death and disease, what will happen to that little bird?" Anna asks as she inches closer.

"She'll die…she'll get sick and die," I mutter.

"She will get sick. Maybe you aren't so stupid, Emily. Your mind is sick because of this." She motions to the surrounding farm. "Sickness is all around you. It is in you."

"I must rest, Anna," I mumble as I turn for the home. I glance once more to ensure the grave is unmolested. "I buried a man today. Then I watched them pick his skull clean-white."

"It wasn't true, my beauty."

"It was to me. I must rest now."

"Go. Sleep is your friend. Rest your tired mind, Emily."

18.

The sun behind him blinds me to the majority of his face, but his smile beams as he walks through the door of our tiny new residence. The day is fading, but I have spent it cleaning the two-room, cinderblock building of a home. It boasts one large room with a bed, refrigerator, tiny stove-oven, and a tattered table with matching chairs—painted an awful orange, and just big enough for two. The only other room is the bathroom. The toilet and tub both required considerable cleaning, but the water is hot and soaking in the tub earlier was quite enjoyable. The cement flooring is rather cool, I can imagine it'll be miserable come winter if rugs are not thrown down.

"This place looks entirely different!" Kaleb proclaims as he glances about the home.

"You look entirely different. You're completely filthy," I say as he attempts to remove his boots.

"Did you know…" he pauses, struggling to remove the second boot, "that pigs are actually quite athletic?" he asks with a grin.

"I did not," I reply, kneeling to assist with removing his stubborn boot.

"Indeed, they are. They're incredibly fast—outran me every chance they got. They are unbelievably strong. I was knocked over at least a dozen times. And, they can jump. I didn't know swine could jump."

The boot gives way, sending me stumbling backwards with dirt and debris falling about the clean floor. "Sounds like an eventful day."

"I loved it, Emily."

"I hadn't a clue. The grin you're wearing wasn't telling in the slightest."

He moves to me, careful not to soil my clothing with his touch, and kisses my lips. "We've done it. We're here."

"We did," I reply with my eyes sealed. "The bathtub is practically screaming your name, husband of mine."

"That's incredibly rude." He chuckles. "I don't have any clean clothes. We'll have to wash these and—"

"Roberta brought a plethora of trousers, holey socks, and farm shirts. They belonged to their son, Chad.

"His wife has been here?"

"Oh yes. She's very kind. We're joining them for supper tonight. She lent me several gowns of hers too. There a few sizes big but they'll suffice. She's going into a town tomorrow to fetch fresh undergarments and unmentionables."

Kaleb stares with mouth agape for several seconds prior to responding. "Are you going with her? Are you...are you going into the town?"

"Heavens no! That would be petrifying, to say the least." I beat his boots together outside the front door, knocking them free of excessive muck. "Perhaps someday we'll go together. That day is not tomorrow. I need time to take all of this in first."

"Meyrick...or, Emily," he says softly.

"Yes."

"Did you know the Squires' own a television set?"

"What? I hadn't given it any thought." My lips curl uncontrollably into a grin. "Here? In their home?"

He smirks, shrugging his shoulders. "I'm assuming. Where else would they keep a television set? They own a telephone as well."

My gaze settles on my toes as I imagine viewing the television set one day. I'm nearly overwhelmed at the idea of seeing and hearing information simultaneously from a device. "Let's focus on today, my love. There's too much too soon to do more than that."

"I want a television set one day, Meyrick," Kaleb says with conviction. "I truly do."

His words have me giggling. "Me too. I want to see it...and I, I would like to visit not only the town Roberta speaks of, but many towns. I want to see all the faces and fascinating things now that we can."

"Me too," he replies—his eyes glistening.

"Our walls will be clad with books. Our children will run and play, their voices filling the evening sky. And, my love, we will have our very own television set."

"And Jennet?" His gaze narrows.

"The instant we have the means, we'll send for her. We will get her here too, I promise."

I'm lifted from the ground in a monstrous hug and twirled in a circle. "We're going to get everything we said we would, Mey—dammit! Emily."

We chuckle as I'm returned to the ground. "I'm quite fond of Emily. I know it's difficult, but I'm going to need you to keep trying."

"I will. I'll do anything for you."
***

"Meyrick!"

I awake in the sitting room to Leroy's voice.

"Dammit, Meyrick. Why the hell is a whole heap of my britches left wet as a trout's twat out in the goddamned yard?"

I prop myself on the divan, attempting to regain my wits. "I apologize...I..."

"I don't need no apology, woman. I need my britches hung and dried so I can shove my balls in 'em when the time comes. Why the fuck is they still out in the basket? What the hell have you been doin' all damn day?"

The images of the burial, the imaginary ravens, and their carnage begin to flood my brain—bringing about a visceral reaction. Leaping from the couch, I scurry around Leroy and to the restroom. I make it to the commode just in time to expel the tea I'd consumed before lying down to rest.

With my elbows resting on the toilet lid, my lip still quivering, I hear Leroy from the doorway.

"Well, I guess that'd explain it. I had the shits this morning, too. I hope like hell you didn't give us the bug with your cookin'."

"I hope...I hope you're feeling better, Leroy."

"I am. In fact, I found my appetite. Once you get them britches sorted, you can heat a skillet."

The first step outdoors is a cautious one. The remainder of the wash is hung to dry in a hasty manner. Although I'm confident the gravesite is intact and as I left it, I avoid looking across the yard because I'm unsure if my mind will allow me to see it that way.

Task complete, I make my way to the kitchen to find Leroy preparing a beverage.

"Ain't no one been out here today, have they?"

"Pardon?" I ask, rummaging through the refrigerator for meal ideas.

"Have you seen Henson's missing hand? That asshole was at the feed-mill, fit to be tied. He ain't gonna let that one go."

"No. No one's been here, Leroy."

"Good. That's damn good. I don't need Henson's crazy ass fussin' and carryin' on over here, too. Not after I just got the other shitstorm settled."

After setting several items on the table, I make my way to the sink to wash my hands. "Do you think it's settled, Leroy? Do you think we're safe?"

He chuckles lowly into his glass. "We're safer than any of them motherfuckers come around here trying to prove otherwise. Put enough of the sonsofbitches in the ground and they'll eventually learn." His eyes, grimy and bloodshot red, cast a gaze rich with an angered excitement.

"Do you think he'll find him, Leroy?"

"Find who?"

"Do you think that Henson fellow will find his missing farm-hand?"

Leroy shrugs from the bistro chair motions for a fresh drink. "I got no clue. Farmhands are about as loyal as flies on horse shit. They up n' leave soon as it dries out. There's no tellin' where that pretty boy's at."

"Did you know him, Leroy? The farm-hand?" I ask softly as I take his empty glass.

He eyes me, jaw unhinged and moving about as if he's gnawing the air. "No. Nah, I didn't know that pansy-ass little shit. Not 'cept for being Henson's hand."

I pour his drink, thick and strong.

"What difference would that make?" he asks as the glass is delivered to his stingy grasp.

"It doesn't, I guess. Just asking."

Supper made, Leroy fed, and dishes put away, I pour him one last drink before he retires to the room to succumb to the toxins coursing through his body.

Two sandwiches are prepared hastily. I collect them with a few other provisions and make my way to Anna and Q.

Entering the barn, I find them gazing out the door on the opposite side. Two lovers with nothing but the blanket of stars creeping slowing to tuck them in…how liberating.

"Hello," I say softly.

"Emily, join us. The night is beautiful…so peaceful," Anna says as she motions me to them.

"I really can't stay long. I brought you something in case you're hungry."

"So thoughtful. Thank you. Are you feeling better, my beautiful?"

The evening is inhaled deeply—fills my lungs to the brim. "Now. I'm fine now."

Anna smiles in the dying light. "It is okay, you know? It is okay to be not okay. Fine is okay, too."

I merely nod and smile in appreciation of her comment.

"All will be well soon."

"I really must go. If Leroy awakens—"

"Soon, my beauty," she repeats. "You will shed him from your mind and never say that name again."

"Anna—"

"Soon."

***

"That was absolutely delicious. Thank you," I proclaim, wiping my mouth.

"I couldn't agree more," Kaleb confirms.

The Squires' home is lovely. The white exterior of the two-story house is in desperate need of scraping and painting. Yet, there's something heartening in its flaws—something soothing about the walls around me.

"Wasn't much," Roberta replies. Roberta Squires is a humble woman. Her hair parts down the middle like a silver stream splitting two light-brown fields and is collected in a braid in the back. She appears as genuine as her tarnished smile.

Their home is well-kept. Pictures and books are dusted. Comfy quilts are folded neatly on the divan. The china cabinet boasts beautiful porcelain and silver cutlery. The home is rich in a happy history, and although modest, it flaunts many man-made possessions that the homes of my community display ungenerously.

"Help me understand something," Roberta continues. "You all speak so eloquently and your vocabularies are like a gosh-darn living Webster to folks in these parts. What kind of schooling did ya'll attend back home?"

The thought of the Community or having to describe any pieces of it has me squirming.

"Education is of high priority back home," Kaleb chimes in. "Reading and arithmetic, science and history. It's all about the foundation."

"Yes. A child's education is important. Tell me…if you're not Amish—"

"Roberta," Daniel interjects.

"They came here—to Idaho," she continues. "I'm curious as to why. I'm only looking for a bit of back-story."

"We did leave, ma'am," I stammer. Under the table I pinch my leg to quell my nerves. "We wish to never return and hope one day our children find the description of our community as odd as you do." My

words quiver as they leave me. "We may be ignorant to much of the world around us but certain evils are universally recognizable." My reply silences the dim-lit dining room for several seconds.

"Amen," Roberta mutters—her eyes glistening. "He works in mysterious ways."

"He does, indeed," Daniel adds. "Emily."

Hearing that name from his mouth has me jumping in my chair. "Yes sir?"

"Are you needing to make a phone call, dear? Long-distance don't come cheap but if you're quick about it we might can work it out come payday."

"Phone call?"

"You been eye-ballin' that phone since you sat down."

My grin is of both embarrassment and excitement. "I've never...forgive me. I've never actually seen a telephone before." The statement leaves our hosts' mouths agape.

"You ain't ever seen a phone? Never?"

I merely shrug, shaking my head.

"Would you like to?" he asks, motioning toward the ugly, green contraption on a dark-cherry wood stand.

"May I?" Gleefully, I scoot from the table and follow him to the device I've only seen in pictures. He lifts a handle from the main portion and rests it aside my face. An odd buzzing enters my ear and then a clicking as his finger moves with a clear lid-looking object with holes aligned atop numbers. A strange noise is heard, followed by something most peculiar...

"Operator," a woman's voice says through the device and into my ear.

"Oh!" Instantly I'm grinning, returning the handle

to Daniel and giggling with delight as he sets it down.

"Ain't that something?" he asks.

"It truly is. It's magnificent."

Kaleb stands from the table. "Do you think we might have a quick look at the television set?" he asks with an eager grin.

The Squires share a curious glance before unanimously erupting in laughter. "It's in here, kids," says Daniel as we migrate to the sitting room.

"Where is it? I know you have it!" Violent words accost me only inches from my ears.

"Oh!" Scrambling beneath the covers, I attempt to detangle the clustered webs of past and present while protecting my head with any bedding I can grasp. "Please." My pleas muffle through the worn linens.

"Shut the hell up," he snarls. "I done told you I ain't raisin' my hand no more, but woman…"

His pause chills the air. Even under the layers of bedding, my view entirely obstructed, I shudder.

"Woman, you are trying my ever-lovin' patience." He inhales through his nostrils, deep and slow. "Where…the fuck…is it?"

Light trickles in from under the sheets. Hot breath—fast and uncontrollable on the back of my hand…one eye blinded by the bedding, the other watches as his shadow nears.

"I won't ask again—"

"Beneath the flooring," I mutter, clinching my eyes closed as the covers are ripped away aggressively. Each inch of my being screams for leniency as the cool air wafting over me sirens my exposure.

"What did you just say?" He towers over me—stone-hard and aching to pounce.

"The kitchen. Beneath the linoleum."

I lie motionless, wondering if his diminishing footsteps and the ruckus that follows in the kitchen will be the last sounds my mind digests.

"You idiot. You stupid idiot…" His low growl from the kitchen has me sinking within myself.

The morning light has yet to pierce the night through the window. I'm oblivious to the time.

He storms back into the room, photograph in hand. "This woulda done got us both killed, Meyrick," he says. "If he found this, you got any clue what that sonofabitch would do to the two of us? Nah, you don't, 'cause you's a piss-ignorant, selfish bitch."

"I had to," I plead, raising my head from the mattress.

"Had to?" he screams.

"Yes. You left it lying on the floor. I was…I was too scared to bring it to you, but knew it was dangerous, so I hid it."

My pathetic explanation squints his gaze—has him analyzing me for several seconds before he's shaking his head. "Nah, I don't buy it." He paces. "I'd like to…hell, I'd even love to, but there's too much to risk here, Meyrick. I got my own neck to worry bout and I can't do that with a manipulative, crazy as hell she-devil trying to get me strung up." His pace stalls…his stare falls to mine.

"Leroy…"

"It won't hurt. I swear to ya. It won't hurt." Nodding as he speaks, his words come calmly—yet sternly. My death is imminent.

"I understand." I whimper as tears dot my gown and me moves to me, positioning his hands as if to strangle me. "Leroy, please."

"It's happening! Now!"

"Not this way! Leave me my breath!"

Stepping backwards, he casts a dumbfounded stare. "What?"

"Am I not worth a bullet? Or even the quick thrust of a blade?" My voice nearly succumbs to fear.

"And leave me to clean the goddamned shit up? Hell no!"

"The barns!" I shriek. "Take me beyond the barns and end me there."

After several seconds he turns for the kitchen. "Get up."

Walking from the home is slightly liberating. Knowing, by some set of circumstances, I'll never again be required to answer to his beckoning is nearly uplifting. As we walk through the stillness, two lonely souls marching into the dark, my teary gaze is affixed on the smallest of the barns. The only chance at reprieve is tucked within those shabby walls. One hand on my shoulder, his other totes a blade I've used to prepare many a meal of his.

Pathetic—to be led away and tended to like a lame mare. As we near, my legs shake under my weakening core.

"Round the back," he mumbles.

"Please."

"This way, Meyrick—"

"Leroy, please. In the barn. I want to go inside."

He halts, turns to me. "Why?"

"I'm scared," I whisper—tasting the salt of my tears as they flood from above. "Lay me down in the hay. Please."

Without response, he opens the door to near-complete darkness and motions me to step inside. My gaze bounces about wildly for any sign of Anna as I enter the barn. There is nothing more than moonlight spotlighting an empty bed of hay—my final resting place.

My breath leaves me in pitiful sobs at the realization that I am going to die. Regretting all previous contemplations of ending my own misery, I'd now beg for a pardon if I felt even a sliver of optimism.

He approaches me—a vague silhouette in the dark building, as my knees nearly buckle and my cries escape.

"Aw, now. Come on. Don't…don't do that…you're a tough little gal. Don't do this." His tone not only lacks hostility, but it's nearly soothing, reason enough to beg.

"I don't want to die, Leroy," I whimper as I crash to the hay beneath me. "I'll do anything, I promise, please."

"I hate you," he replies coldly from above, his face unidentifiable in the dark. "I hate you because…" his voice strains. *Could it be?* Could this be remorse? "I hate you because I love you, Meyrick."

"Leroy, please…spare me. I won't, I wouldn't. Whatever it is you believe I'm conspiring, I'm not. I promise you. Please don't kill me. I don't want to die!" I beg. When pleading for one's life, dignity is nonexistent.

"Damn you, Meyrick." He turns from me. Perhaps his walls are crumbling.

While repositioning myself amongst the dampened hay, my hand rests upon a familiar object. Cold and hard, the mallet lies where I left it after bludgeoning the fellow who attempted to own me in this very place.

"There's no trust. I got no trust for you. I can't...dammit, I want to, but you keep at it!"

I should stand, mallet in hand, and strike down my executioner, yet I am still.

"What...what is this, Meyrick?" he asks from the shadows.

"What is what—"

"Bread or...or, are these... Them hands is still here, ain't they!" His rage fills the barn. "Fresh fuckin' sandwiches just laying round out here! Don't tell me them hands ain't still here!"

My words are frozen within me. They left the meals I prepared them. They've left them to rot with me.

From the left, she slinks silently beside me. Her hand, a warm serpent, slides atop mine to grip the mallet. "Anna—"

"Ssshhh, my beauty. Run."

I remain petrified as she stands with the mallet in her grasp.

"What in god's name—" Leroy's wails detonate within the tiny barn. They enter my ears with maddening ferocity as the mallet meets his foot.

"Run!" Anna screams.

"You bitch! You're dead!" Leroy's threats come closer as he hobbles through the dusty darkness toward us.

"Stand! Get up and run, Emily!"

Her warning, although distinct, lacks a sense of realism—as if I'm floating on my knees and watching from afar. I spring to life as Leroy topples to the dirty floor, bellowing out in agony. The barn's open backdoor frames a star-speckled canvas. I dart into the night, unsure of which direction to run.

"Emily!" Anna calls from behind.

"Where?" I ask frantically. "Where do I go?"

"Run! Run from here."

"What of Leroy? Will you end him?"

"It cannot end tonight. You know it does not end tonight."

"What? Anna—"

"Run!"

Without any further attempt to digest the situation, I turn from Anna and Leroy's howling suffering and dash into the surrounding vegetation. Unlike the thick, plush foliage surrounding the woodland, here the waist-high brush is coarse and longs to poke and prod. I enter, biting my bottom lip and holding my arms well above my midriff. Each step is increasingly agonizing as if all the thorny parts of the shrubbery are aiming for me deliberately. They slide across my legs and hips with searing intention until I've cleared them and am free to move briskly through the tall grass leading to the meadow. Free to move, but to where? There is nowhere to run. I'm alone in an untamed world of wild eyes watching from the dark. "Damn you, Anna…damn you!"

Before me is a vast open, now graced by the promise of dawn on the far horizon. Behind me are the wails of Leroy and all that is left of my existence. Behind me offers the only definitive outcome, and it is not an option.

An uncaged lovebird tossed to the sky, I am free to fly but lack destination and am certain to flutter directly into peril.

The morning is madness, complete and utter

insanity, and I'm confident my mind isn't to blame for this chaos. I run to the light. I run until his voice has drowned under the waves of tractor motors and singing birds. I run until I can't feel the sensation of my legs hammering the soft earth beneath me any longer and the burning within my chest is no longer uncomfortable but blackening to my vision. I run until I meet a tree line. Rich and vast, the trees summon me like old friends—my only friends. I slide into them like a turkey into a cornfield and instantly my anxiety lessens. The calming effects are just enough that I may physically recuperate from the escape efforts.

There are no trails here. Here there are only limbs reaching for one another. The forest holds the chill of the morning air. Maneuvering through the denseness I eventually come to a clearing.

Downed trees adorned with various mushrooms cover the opening of the forest floor. I spy an area plush with green grass aside a tall, thick tree and I contemplate a brief rest. The sense of sanctuary is shattered as the sound of a vehicle motor echoes from beyond the trees on the other side of the clearing.

Fear grasps my breath. Affixed as the trees around me, I listen to the engine grumbling closer. *It isn't him.* "It…it isn't him." Whatever it is that creeps along whatever road is on the other side of those trees is not Leroy.

Initially I remain motionless. The realization that whomever is approaching might be willing to rescue me is originally disregarded—trampled by fear of the unknown. The reality that I am alone and a madman will undoubtedly be hunting me forces me to take the initial step. The engine's mumbling intensifies and I realize I'll need to race for the road if I'm to flag the driver down.

Over and through the trees I scurry, knowing I could be rushing directly toward any number of Leroy's enemies. Their comrades could be planted about the same farm I've just fled—their bodies tossed in shabby, shallow graves.

I leap onto the dirt road from the woodland just as a pristine truck approaches and screeches to a crunching halt. Dust encircles me in a suffocating cloud. It clears, leaving me staring down a beautiful brown pickup—its driver tucked inside. For several seconds I'm left to ponder the decision I've made. Worst-case-scenarios dance about in my mind and just as I've convinced myself I've made a detrimental mistake, the door opens.

"Are you okay?" asks an ash-haired gentleman. He's tall, distinguished-looking, and undeniably handsome.

I remain silent as he approaches guardedly. "Are you okay?"

"No," I choke out. "I need help." My words have him nodding his head. "Can you help me?"

"Yes, my dear. Yes, I can."

19.

"Dear, if you'll just take a seat." Roberta ushers me in front of a weathered vanity within the master bedroom. "You have the loveliest hair. My mother loved to braid my hair." Her fingers work their way through my messy locks. "Did your mother tend to your hair, child?"

Evaluating my expression within the oval mirror before me, I attempt to appear unguarded as I prepare my response. "I don't remember, ma'am. I do not believe so."

She says nothing initially as she reaches for a soft-bristled brush and methodically brushes my hair from scalp to tip. "I believe 'up' will be most appropriate for the service," she says softly.

"Service?"

"Sunday's sermon. We'll have your hair up when we introduce you and Kaleb to the congregation."

Her confident proclamation has me churning inside. The thought of congregating in any church is dizzying. A foul nausea wets my mouth and forehead and squeezes my innards.

"Are you okay, dear? You don't look good."

"I think I'm going to be ill."

Roberta steps aside as I reach for a small wastebasket near the vanity.

"Oh...dear. Nausea of a morning. How peculiar."

"Excuse me. I'm going to be ill."

My eyes open to a foreign setting. Flinging forward, I find I'm not nauseated in the slightest. Comfortable bedding, thick and heavy, drapes my legs as I glance about the room attempting to recall my whereabouts.

The room is lavished with fine furnishings—things that could come directly from the pages of one of Jennet's silly glossy magazines.

The lamp next to the bed, as well as the nightstand it sits atop, are easily of higher quality than any furniture piece in Leroy's home. I could dust and polish the worn stands and tables daily but next to these they'd be rubbish.

The room smells of pine and the walls are a deep, rich wood. The bed I'm in is undoubtedly the most comfortable bed I've ever slept in and the abnormally large clock on the wall states the time is two-thirty-eight in the afternoon. A sense of security has me contemplating snuggling into the luxurious bedding and drifting away once more. A budding curiosity— who are my hosts exactly, has me peeling the blankets away reluctantly.

The cold marble flooring beneath my feet gives a feeling of insignificance as I slide from the sheets. The room and home are indeed grand, but something about the large, square aqua tiles is prodigious.

The nightgown I'm wearing is the softest cotton. I could wear this daily if that were optional. I open the bulky wooden door to a bright hallway aligned with great windows and potted plants. The afternoon's warmth is amplified within the hall as the sun shines through. I walk along the tiled hallway—the aqua-green path to the remainder of this gorgeous home. So still is the grand corridor, even my breath seems to reverberate.

Through the windows I see a well-kept yard of thick, trimmed grass surrounded by countless trees encapsulating the home. Nearing the end of the hallway spawns an odd feeling, like approaching or lingering the outskirts of a conversation uninvited.

I remain there a moment more before bashfully pulling on the brass handle to peek through. A heavy scent of vanilla, cinnamon and butter wafts as I pull the door open completely. "Hello?" I gently call out over a bulky sitting room of fine, leather furniture. The room also smells of whisky and pipe-tobacco. Although it's reminiscent of my father, I find it oddly comforting.

Assuming I've been unheard, I step inside to follow this marble river further. The sweet scents of baking goods have my mouth wet with hunger.

"Hello there."

"Oh!" I shriek, startled at the gentle voice of a young woman, likely around my age.

She grins—a smile that assures me she finds the encounter as awkward as I. "I didn't mean to startle you. Are you…you must be Emily?"

I nod politely, remain poised, and move closer to offer a sociable handshake.

"My name is Becca. I live here."

She's gorgeous. I immediately assume her to be of similar unfortunate circumstances. Her long, dark-brown hair is pulled back neatly, exposing her flawless ivory face and green eyes. Her apron bears no signs of baking—no flour or yolk.

"We're likely the same size. I'll find you some comfy jeans and a t-shirt if you're cool with that?"

"Cool?" I mutter.

She giggles and motions me to sit. The sofa, although grand and lovely, is cold and feels constricted as if it could pop beneath me as I sit.

"I'm not a baker, but it's the thought that counts,

right?"

It is only when she turns away that I notice she's dressed in denim blue-jeans. The clothing is form-fitting and accentuates her thighs and rear-end. I've seen a few women in unflattering work pants, but these are anything but unflattering. She returns, toting a cinnamon-roll on a small plate and a glass of milk. Attempting to process the scene is difficult. I want to enquire further so that I might gauge if she's liberated in her choice of attire. Likely, however, my rescuer is another monster who requires his pleasurers wear specific articles of clothing while tending to his every whim.

"Here's the final product. Hope it doesn't kill ya," she says nonchalantly as she sets the saucer and glass before me.

"Kill me?"

"Ha. Yeah. I'm not much in the kitchen. I took a home-economics class in high school. Teach had the hots for me so I passed with a C. I burned everything, even the cookies for the annual charity drive. But I love these rolls in a can."

"A can?"

"I see you've met my daughter?" The ash-haired gentleman enters the room.

I stand immediately. "Hello, sir."

"Like I said, please, call me Earl. And this is Rebecca—"

"Becca," the girl boldly asserts.

"Becca." Earl kisses her head before seating himself. The interaction is distressingly abnormal to me. Had I corrected my father in such a manner, especially in the presence of a guest, the consequences would be astronomical.

"Please, Emily, don't feel obligated to stand. Please sit," Earl says kindly.

I seat myself as Becca sits beside her father.

"Emily," Earl continues, "I need you to know a few things." He positions himself to the edge of the couch, seated directly across from me. "You are under no obligation to tell us anything immediately. Take the day to rest. You are safe here." He nods while speaking, as if to add emphasis. "Whatever circumstances brought you here…whoever hurt you, they can't hurt you here." There's an intensity in his voice and gaze. "When you're ready, you can talk to me or Becca about anything you like."

I merely nod politely.

"What do you need right now?" he adds.

"I'd like to bathe," I say, almost reflexively. "If it's okay, I'd like to bathe before I go."

Earl smiles kindly. "Of course. There are several guest bathrooms."

"Emily," Becca interjects, "there's really no need for you to rush off. You're hurt. We'll get ya fed, get ya bathed, and then I'll have a look at you," she says before patting her father's shoulder and standing.

"A look at me? I don't quite understand."

"Becca here is a medical student. One more year and she'll be an actual doctor," Earl proclaims proudly with a grin.

"A doctor? You're to be a physician? A medical physician?" I ask as a smile creeps across my face as well.

"That's right. I'll start my residency in sixteen months."

"That's amazing. That's absolutely outstanding." I stand, looking toward Becca in awe.

"Are you okay, dear?" Earl asks. It isn't until he questions that I realize I've shed a few tears.

"I am. I've never met someone…and you're a woman. You're so, strong…" My voice strains. "It's truly amazing. I'm honored to be in your presence."

Rather than flattered, Becca tilts her head and appears somewhat concerned. She smiles politely while studying me. "You've never met a woman medical student?" she asks softly. "Is that what you're saying, Emily?"

I retake my seat on the cold-cushioned sofa and attempt to saddle my admiration. "I've yet to meet an actual medical physician, man or woman," I say confidently. "I am beyond honored, that my first encounter is with you. You have no idea what this means to me."

Becca and Earl stare blankly, as if my words have drained them of emotion. Becca nods after a few seconds. "So, you've never been examined by a licensed physician before?" she asks.

I merely shake my head.

"Well, there's always a first, right? I'll show you to the restroom."

***

"May I come in?" Becca's voice asks from the other side of the guest-bedroom door.

"Certainly." I remain seated on the bed, legs crossed and hands clasped.

"How was your bath?" She enters the room cautiously.

"I enjoyed it. I've never bathed in a tub larger than

me. This home is quite extravagant."

She smiles as she sits next to me. "The sundress fits okay?"

"It does indeed. If I may tend to my clothing, I'll be on my way the instant it's dry—"

"What happened out there, Emily?" Becca's soft hand takes mine. "I won't hurt you. My dad isn't going to hurt you. We just want to help. But you gotta talk to me. My dad can help you."

"Is your father a farmer?"

"He is."

"He hires farmhands to tend to his needs?"

She sighs passively. "He does. But we can talk about employment after we—"

"Once my wash has dried, I'll be on my way. I have much ground to cover and wish to be as far from here as possible."

"I see. I'll just check on your clothes."

"There isn't a hand who does that for you?" Although my tone lacks cynicism, it's taken her aback.

"Emily, my dad loves and respects everyone who works for him. He came here with his mother from Manitoba when he was thirteen. He built his life from nothing."

"He's Canadian?"

"Yes, he is. Is that where you're from originally, Emily?"

I nod.

"Good. And you came here for work, yes?"

Initially I hesitate, but offer an additional nod after a few seconds.

"I see. Many people come to the farming states for work. And you…you came here all by yourself? That must have been scary."

Her question dampens my eyes instantly. It has me teetering on the brink of an emotional topple. "Please. May we speak of this later?"

"Yes," she replies promptly. "Later. Emily." She secures my hand once more. "I'm not asking you to trust me right away. I know that's too much to ask right now. But I need you to hear me. You're safe here. Whoever did this to your face and had you running through the woods, scared for your life, they'd know better than to come looking for you here, even if they knew you were here. You're safe. I promise."

As I wipe my tears away, I remember how soft the bed beneath me is, how I'd melted into it like warm butter.

"But if you gotta go, if you really want to leave, I can take you wherever you need to go. But I really wish you'd stay."

"May I rest?" I ask softly. "My mind is so weary. I feel as though my mind could sleep for years and years. I know that's senseless but if I'm as safe as you claim, let me just…rest."

Her smile is genuine. My words have made her happy and that's showing on her face. Jennet would smile in such a way on our walks during reckless conversations. Perhaps I'm being reckless now, but I coming to trust this woman.

"Rest. Rest all you want. I'll peek in around supper time and if you're awake, perfect, if not I'll check in around breakfast."
   ***

There's nothing left to clean. I scan our little home fervently but it's as tidy as can be expected for what it is. Kaleb will arrive within hours to track in muck and leave a glass setting about—shed his work clothes and toss them to the floor carelessly. He'll keep my mind preoccupied with meaningless tasks. For now, however, my thoughts are consumed with faces I have yet to see—countless smiles and condemning gazes peering my way. Peeling my sins back like scabs with their eyes to delight in my vulnerability—pink and oozing and screaming at the exposure. The congregation...Roberta claims they're welcoming and holy but I'm certain the book they preach from is remarkably similar to the book my community sits upon. The things they'll take without so much as unclasping their hands. It's inescapable, I'll be amongst them sequentially. The thought is near maddening and has me pacing.

I long to see the world and its diversity. I wish to hear languages my mind cannot process and taste food completely foreign to my mouth. I want to learn of religion, but I no longer wish to practice it. I wish to pray, but under the roof of my choosing. To sit in a room, incased in conviction and stanch with standardization, opposes my new ideals. In one day, I'll be ushered through the church doors. This is the cruelest.

"Emily," Roberta's voice calls from outside. The hint of hysteria in her tone has me opening the door hastily as she's barging through.

"Roberta? Are you okay?"

"There's been an accident at the barn. You best get on up to the house." Her withered expression is laced with panic and perspiration.

"Kaleb!"

"We best get on up—"

"Tell me my husband is okay, Roberta!" I demand, gown clutched on my thighs within blanched-white fists.

"He fell, Emily. He got banged up pretty good. Leg's busted." She shrugs. "It's busted pretty good."

"Busted?" I ask in a whisper.

"It's broken," she replies with conviction. "We best get up there. He's hollerin' for ya."

The brisk walk to the Squires' home is wretchedness. The thought of his misery is unbearable. I hear his wailing as we approach the home and it craters my soul.

Inside I find him splayed on the floor, his foot atop a worn pillow and his face grimaced in agony staring upward. Trousers torn to just below the knee reveal an undeniably malformed right ankle. Parts of it are robin's egg blue, and others a deep purple—like an angry sky before it storms. His breath is rapid and sporadic, controlled by pain.

"Kaleb!" I rush to his side, falling to my knees. "Kaleb, I'm here."

"Meyrick! It's too much…the pain."

Tears stream along the sides of his dusty face, leaving etch marks as they move slowly to dampen the pillow his head rests upon.

"Please," I ask sternly, "do you have anything for him? Do you have medicine?"

My question elicits an impassive glance between the Squires before Daniel calmly exits the room. The only means I have to comfort my husband are gentle words and grasping his trembling hand. I've never felt smaller.

"This here's pretty potent stuff," Daniel proclaims upon reentry. He totes a small, brown elixir bottle, bearing no label. "You handle your liquor, boy?"

"What?" I snap. "He doesn't drink liquor."

"Oh. Well this here ain't no Tylenol or—"

"Tylenol?" I interject. "Do you have curcumin or turmeric...if you must, use aspirin, but he's never used such medicines before."

"Meyrick," he mutters. "Help me. I can't."

"What do you mean, never had an aspirin? I ain't never met a person who's not had an aspirin. I couldn't make a day without it," Daniel states. "But I don't think that's gonna do the trick. Roberta's gonna have to reset that leg. That boy's gonna need more than an aspirin."

"The bottle," I say definitively, wiping his tears. "Give him the bottle. Is it liquor or—"

"Oh no," Daniel chuckles as he pours a spoonful of the elixir. "He won't feel nothing soon enough."

"The sooner the better," I reply as my husband's quivering lips enclose the spoon.

"He might want two—"

"That'll do, Daniel," Roberta snarls. "Once the lights go out, we'll get that leg set. We'll get him moved out to the small-house to settle."

"You feel it's okay to move him? Shouldn't he stay put for now?" I ask, still holding his hand.

"Young lady, if this man is to maintain his dignity, he'll need to be in the company of his wife alone until he's healed up enough to get up and around. Nature don't take breaks. It's best we get him back to the small-house where you can tend to him."

"I understand."

As his breathing slows, his grip lessens, I find myself conflicted internally. I would take his pain instantly. I would fight alongside him or die for him. Yet, knowing his suffering will pardon me, if only temporarily, from the clutches of any congregation has me feeling graced with a sense of reprieve.

Roberta collects her things to mend while I remain stationary with my thoughts. I watch the pain leave his expression as the elixir works its way into him—relief washing over his face as he slips away...hopefully to somewhere pleasant.

20.

"I was born in this home. I came two weeks early and the snow covered the roads. Dad says his fingers bled that night. He chewed his nails down too far. My mother said it was awful but I came just a few hours after her water broke."

I sit across from Becca at the dining table, listening to her history and basking in the normalcy. It's nearly seven in the evening. She hasn't mentioned my departure, neither have I. I'm content to sleep another night in this restful place.

"Your mother?" I ask before blowing on the tomato soup before me to cool it.

"Washington. She left before I started high school."

"I'm sorry."

"Don't be. She was a total bitch."

So taken aback am I by this statement, that I set my spoon aside and remain speechless.

"What?" she asks, chuckling. "Your parents may have been pillars but my mother was awful."

"Pillars?"

"Pillars of society."

"I'm familiar with the term. Your father…does he know you feel this way about your mother?"

Becca nods while sipping her tea. "Oh yeah. He hates her too. And for good reason. The whore cheated on the poor guy more times than he can count. She just…left one night. Good riddance."

I continue observing her casual declaration while a fire burns from my core out.

"She gave me life. I owe her that and what not. I guess I could be more respectful but—"

"I hate my father," I say somberly.

Several seconds pass with our stares locked before she nods. "Okay. Okay then."

"I'm sorry," I mutter.

"No. No, this is good. You can tell me if you want." Her soft reply has me feeling safe—the safest I've felt in a while.

"I hate him. I hate everything about him and his people…my people."

Her intense observation assures me she's devouring every word. "And your mother. Do you hate your mother?"

"No. I loved her."

"Loved?"

"She's gone. She left."

"Left? She left to where, Emily?"

"The trees." My response perplexes her. Her eyes squint as she gently bites her bottom lip. "She ran away into the trees."

"Emily, is your mother out there too? We need to help her—"

"No. She left my home…my home in Canada…my community, and ran to the trees. They all run into the trees, those who leave. They never come home."

"Is that how you left? You ran away, into the trees?"

"No. Yes…somewhat. My friend was waiting to take me away with a vehicle."

"Your father, he was the one who hurt you. Did he do that to your face?"

"No." My shoulders tense as if my father is standing just behind me—his breath on my ear. "I don't want to talk about this anymore."

Becca smiles. Although she nods in agreement, her

gaze hungrily craves additional details.

"May I stay here awhile longer, Becca?"

"Yes. That'd actually make me happy. You like it here?"

I sigh, reaching for my spoon. "I like feeling how I do now."

"And how is that, Emily?"

"Sheltered."

***

Many of the garments displayed on the bed are quite brazen by my typical standard. Some of the dresses lack appropriate shoulder coverage. Some do not fall completely to the ankle. As I skim through them, I find the brashest of the gowns and set them aside—I'll start with these. I too wish to feel liberated.

Gowns in the closet and bedsheets pulled down, I take a moment to ingest the situation. The feeling of security is all but drowned by the aching sense of responsibility.

"She told me to run." Anna. I wonder where she's sleeping now. If she's sleeping. I wonder if she's breathing now…if Leroy is breathing.

I've said before that I am no savior, yet I find Anna and Q heavy on my mind as I slip into the cool bedding. Cunning and deadly, Anna has proven she's capable of defending herself—much more capable than I.

Just as I bring the sheets to my chin, a knock on the door has me sitting forward. "Hello?"

His friendly face slides through the opening door. "Do you have everything you need?" Earl asks.

"I do," I reply bashfully.

"I hear you'll be sticking around a while." He steps into the room, opening the door completely as he does.

"It's only temporary. I can depart—"

"Actually," he interjects, "I was needing your help with something."

"You…need *my* help?" I reply skeptically.

"You're an educated woman, Emily. You speak articulately and what not. The thing is…a few of my employees could sharpen their reading and writing skills." He perches on the edge of an elegant chair near the door. "They know the basics, but if you could help them along, I know they'd be eager for the opportunity."

"You're asking me to teach them?"

"Yes."

My smile comes instantly and is uncontainable. "Yes. I would love to be of assistance. It's the least I can do."

The sound of his hands slapping his knees solidifies the agreement. "That settles it then." He stands and strolls toward the door. "Becca will work out the details tomorrow. We'll get ya set up with whatever you need and get ya on the payroll—"

"Oh, I couldn't possibly take payment from you. I owe you so much already."

"Nonsense. We're glad to have you here, and you'll be performing a service," he asserts confidently. "We interviewed a tutor just last week. Sweet as pie but didn't have the gumption. This couldn't be better timing."

I search my brain—scour it for the appropriate words, yet I'm left shrugging and grinning in appreciation. "Thank you. Thank you so much."

"Thank you, Emily."

As he exits, the door closing softly behind him, I

slide into the bedding awaiting the ceiling to crash down or the walls to topple in on me. If this contentment is genuine, surely it will be followed by something dreadful.

***

He's never snored louder. His burdened breath fills our tiny quarters from the bed yet I am thankful his pain has ceased, if only temporarily. Several pillows prop his splinted leg. Swollen toes protrude from the bandaging—pale grapes in a row.

I'm uneducated as to how long bones take to heal as I've yet to tend to one. His injury will have him bedbound for weeks no doubt.

The soft amber glow of the lamp illuminates his complexion and reflects in the tiny beads of sweat adorning his brow. I dread the moment he awakens to agony. He's been resting for hours and I'm certain the instant the effects of the tonic fade, his anguish will rile.

The night will be sleepless. With a stool next to the bed, I sit and prepare for an evening of vigilant watch. No sooner am I seated than a gentle knocking is heard at the door—gently as a jay tapping on glass.

I open the door to a somber-looking Roberta. "Please come in. He's still sleeping soundly."

"That goop'll keep him under until morning. We can load him up another spoon full if need be." Roberta steps inside. "He might need it for the road."

"Road?"

My enquiry is initially ignored. She wanders to the bed and my sleeping husband and her answer comes in her footsteps—hesitant and foreboding.

"We must leave here. That's what this is...yes?"

"What is your name? He called you Meyrick. Is that

a middle name, or your maiden name or an alias? Who are you?"

I stand proud before my husband at the bedside. "My name is Emily McCormick. I told you this the day we met."

Her soft chuckle and diverted gaze assure me my dignity is the only thing I'm pleading for. "I left my name when we left our home. We wanted to start anew. I wanted something untarnished, and so I left my name and took another."

"Ya know," she shakes her finger, "a good gardener knows how to spot a weed. Even the prettiest wildflowers are weeds."

"We only wanted a new life—"

"Ya came here, expecting a child, lied about who ya was and now he can't work. He got laid up right out the chute," she snaps, our gazes finally connecting. "You'll have tonight."

"And then? Where are we to go then?"

"That isn't my concern."

"Please. Roberta, we aren't scoundrels. Where will we go from here?"

After several seconds, nothing more than Kaleb's snores to fill the silence, she replies, "A fella will be by, early morning. He'll take the two of ya. I don't know which farm you'll end up on or—"

"Kaleb can't work. What are we to do?"

"As I've already said, that isn't my concern." From her jacket pocket, she retrieves the brown elixir bottle, it's oily contents glimmer in the lamp's glow as she sets on the wooden stool. "He'll need this. Careful with it. Ride'll be here round sunup."

"That should allow you ample time to prepare for

your Sunday's service...God's work and all."

Halfway out the door she turns, an angry shrew of a woman. "We owe you nothin', you ungrateful, dishonest little swindler."

I step to her, fists balled and gaze hazy with tears. "Sleep well, Roberta."

***

"Hello. Emily? Emily who are you talking to?"

My blinking eyes don't initially focus. An odd voice has me looking about frantically on a strange scene. Upright yet unsteady, I spin to return to Kaleb but the door behind me is not the door to the Squires' small-house.

"Emily. Are you okay?" the woman asks once more from behind.

"No, Roberta!" I reply heatedly, turning to face her. "I am...not..."

"Emily, it's Becca. Are you okay?"

My hand on the doorknob, standing partially in the windowed corridor and partially in the guest bedroom, my face warms with embarrassment. "I'm sorry. This is...it's humiliating."

"Are you okay now?"

"Yes, I am. I'm simply embarrassed."

"Oh, nonsense. The maid, Beatrice, her picture is in the living-room. Anyways, she used to sleepwalk right out the front door at least once a month clear up into her eighties."

The morning light glares intrusively through the glass. Crisp and bright is the morning sky, yet my brain is wrapped in a thick fog as if I've been starved of sleep for days.

"She's dead now."

"What?" I gasp.

"Beatrice. She died a few years back. Are you about ready for breakfast?"

I merely nod while glancing toward the empty bed. My bandaged husband is not there. He exists only in the ground, bones in a sheet, and in my decomposing psyche.

"You sure you're okay?" she asks once more. "Need a minute or so? Sleepwalking is some bizarre business."

"I'm fine," I stammer as I feel my lungs. "I must look a fright."

"You look ravishing. Let's go get some breakfast."

The scents of breakfast meats and syrup hang heavy in the living room. My reflection in an oval mirror isn't entirely unpresentable. My hair is managed and my face healing.

"Breakfast is on the table now," Becca calls from the dining room.

As I approach, I pause to see a familiar figure perched outside on the ledge of one of three rectangular windows behind the dining table. A bushy, black raven gawks inward on our morning feast splayed out on the long, oak table.

Initially I stand next to Becca as the cook sets a coffee pot down.

"You must be Emily," the older woman says sweetly.

"I am. And you are?" I ask, glancing from her to the window repeatedly.

"I'm Janice. Nice to meet you," the gray-haired, hefty lady says before turning to collect the remainder of the meal.

"Janice has been with us since Beatrice passed—"

"The windows," I stutter.

"I beg your pardon?" Becca seats herself and motions me to do the same. My gaze is now affixed on the visitor lurking just outside.

"The windows in the dining area. They're quite unique…lovely."

"A pain to clean," Janice interjects as she returns with a plate of biscuits and places them centrally.

"Birds?"

"Huh?" Janice responds.

"Are the birds what make a mess of the windows?" I respond, pointing toward the raven.

"Oh, heavens no," Janice says. "I took the birdfeeders and baths down my first week here. I'm not much of a bird person…unless they're fried or boiling in a pot," she adds with a chuckle.

"I agree," Becca follows up—bacon muffling her response as she glares through the window. "Ya never really see birds up by the house. Cats keep 'em run off."

I methodically meander closer to the pane. Not once does my gaze wander from the bird—its beady eye watches my approach from the side. Our stares connect. I watch as the raven bows. It's haggard beak—thick and bowed, points downward. I watch in confusion as the bird's beak curls upward into a sly grin. "Impossible. Literally not possible," I mumble.

"Emily?" Becca says softly from behind me.

"You're not real…just go." I whisper. "If you're not truly here. How can you leave?"

"Emily, is everything okay?"

The curl of the raven's grin intensifies as its head lifts, it's gaze hardens on mine—a horrific little fiction.

"You're not here!" A solid thudding sound resonates as I slap the glass with my palm.

"Emily, what is it?" Becca asks as she moves to join me at the window. Her pupils dance as she looks about the yard and trees.

The raven, its bushy plumage and devilish grin, has vanished when I return my attention to the window once more.

"Nothing I can explain," I mutter vacantly.

"Girl, I think you need some caffeine. What do you take?"

I feel her gaze on the side of my face as physically as a fly as she awaits my response. "Black."

21.

Anna said my brain was ill due to the environment. That theory is slipping. My madness follows me like a sickening shadow. It robs me of my morning smile. This is the ceiling crashing…the walls toppling. Mine is an existence of rubble and havoc.

In the guestroom I've slipped into a form-fitting sundress. I'm incredibly uncomfortable at my exposed shoulders, my arms crisscrossed over my chest so that my palms may cover either of them. This liberation is nearly claustrophobic—I can feel their eyes on me…every member of the Community's searing gaze transfixed on my shoulders. Their mouths agape as they count the tiny freckles along either pale, white scapula—tallying my imperfections.

"Emily?" Becca's voice derails my thought as the doorknob turns. "I'm coming in."

I don't look to her, but to the floor, and use fists of hair to attempt to cover my shoulders as tears fill my eyes.

"Oh, sweetie." She walks to me calmly. "What's wrong?"

"I'm disgraceful. I look like a whore."

"What?" She gasps. "You look stunning. Come sit."

At the vanity she pulls my hair back and secures it with a band, completely exposing my nude shoulders. "May I do your makeup?"

"What? Heavens no."

"You sure?" Her tone is calm and coaxing. "I could do wonders for those bruises. The thing with makeup, it's washable…nothing permanent."

"Okay," I reply with a defeated shrug.

Becca leaves to retrieve her tricks. I'm left to glare at what is left of me. I once fancied what I saw in the mirror. There's not much worth mentioning now.

Becca returns excitedly. Atop the vanity she unzips a green bag and sets out several oddly-shaped tubes and circular disk-like objects. An odd unnatural chemical odor permeates over her supplies. "I am going to fix you right up," she says, standing over me from behind. Her touch is electrically uncomfortable atop my shoulders and has be jolting forward. "I'm sorry."

"It's fine…it's okay."

"This foundation will get you taken care of." The creamy, smooth, flesh-colored substance is applied with her fingers and my markings begin to vanish. The more she adds the less noticeable my greenish bruising is.

She turns me to face her. "I need you to trust me. I'll have you looking like a beauty queen…you're so damned pretty as it is."

"Like the magazines?" I ask as she continues dabbing about my face.

"Magazines?"

"The girls on the magazines. The beauty queens."

"Sure."

"If I don't enjoy what you've done, I'm free to wash it away when you're finished?"

She giggles. "Hold real still and don't blink. You…are free…to do as you please." The tickling on my eyelids is nearly unbearable. "Emily, the mind is a weird thing. It can respond to stress and trauma differently for different folks." Becca reaches for something else. "Open your mouth, no talking." She rolls it over my lips—smooth and velvety. "Press 'em together like this." She eyes me as if I'm a canvas. "Almost done," she chirps happily. "If you're ready to talk about what's happened, I'm good at listening. I know several good—"

"I had a husband, we came here to work. He died. There's nothing more."

She nods passively. "All done."

The girl in the mirror is nearly unrecognizable. I'm unsure if I should smile or scratch this paint from my face and eyes. So pronounced are my features now. My lips, a profounder red, and my injuries have been painted over. It's my eyes, however, that have me mystified. I'm looking into the eyes of a stranger—a magazine girl with black rims accentuating her bold, beautiful eyes. She's beautiful...I look beautiful.

"You're fucking beautiful, Emily," Becca says. "With or without the warpaint. But I wanted you to see this."

"I'm beautiful," I mutter.

"Yes. Gorgeous."

"I was beautiful. I was..."

"So, we can keep the makeup for today—"

"Why are you helping me?" I ask sternly, turning to her in my chair.

Becca cautiously steps backwards. "That's what we do."

"That's what you do?" I snap.

"It's what we've always done. We give back. It's important to my father and it's important to me. When I've completed my residency, I'll be dedicating my career to helping those who cannot help themselves."

Her words have me wanting to bury my face in my palms—to snuff out the confusion. If not for her restorative efforts on my face, I would. "How?"

"How? I'd be working with people who are less fortunate—"

"How are some so kind while others are so disturbingly cruel? How does the spectrum have such a variance? It makes no sense to me, and so I'm left questioning if it's genuine."

"Emily, I only want to help you—"

"Why? You owe me nothing. You gain nothing my aiding me. I am nothing." I stand. "I'll be forever broken, my mind forever fractured. I'll be forever his."

"Stop. Now," Becca asserts. "You are somebody. The sooner you see that, the better off the world will be. No doubt you've got some healing to do, but it can be done. So, do it." Her tone is no longer gentle. "Forever whose? Your father's? Your husband's? Who were you talking about?"

"I don't want to talk about it."

"Do you know that as we speak, my father is out searching the countryside for an employee? He's literally been out looking since eleven o'clock last night. He was searching for him when he found you. He loves the people who work here. He'd do anything for them. He'd do anything for you—"

"Your name! Oh my god," I shriek. "Your last name. It's Henson."

Becca stares blankly. "Yes. Why do you ask? Do you know something about Dane?"

"I must go. I have to leave immediately—"

"You'll do no such thing." Cold and monotone, Becca maneuvers herself between me and the door. "No more games, Emily. What do you know? Where'd you come from?"

"I told you, I don't want to talk—"

"This isn't about you right now. Do you know where Dane is? Tell me now."

"Dane?"

Becca takes my hand aggressively. "Come with me." I'm pulled from the room and through the home until we reach a study room. There, on a grand, dark wood desk, sits a framed photo of familiar faces. There's no denying I recognize the young couple. The instant they fall into view my eyes swell and spill my emotions.

"Emily, please. Tell me where he is. We love this boy."

"I don't know him. I promise."

"Emily—"

"The girl? What happened to the girl?"

"She's dead," Becca whispers. "These two came to Idaho to work on a potato farm. He got sick with a flu and they were tossed out like trash. Ended up on a makeshift farmstead a few miles from here. A place of nightmares from what Dane described."

"How did she—"

"She hung herself after the bastard who took 'em in had his way with her one too many times."

"No."

"Oh yeah. He'd have put a bullet in Dane too had that boy not busted out the cellar they were locked in and run off in the night. Dad found him a lot like he found you." She reaches for the photo frame as her words have me whirling—what is left of my reality is colliding with their tragedy. "Emily!"

I heave my breakfast into the study garbage pail. There's no denying, Dane and his bride fell into the clutches of Leroy. Dane was there to exact revenge and Anna buried a blade in him before he could explain himself.

"Emily…did you come from…do you know this place? Do you know the farmstead I'm speaking of?"

I search my brain for lies. I search my brain for courage. I find neither and therefor simply mutter the truth. "Yes."

"Oh my god. He's the one who did this to you? You were there…how long were you…did he hurt your husband?"

Wiping the retch from my mouth, I look to Becca. "I'm unsure how long."

"Emily, did he kill your husband?"

Tears stream my face as I prepare to speak this truth the first time aloud. "Yes. That bastard killed my husband," I say agonizingly. "He took from me the most precious gift and left me with a rotting crater inside."

"He'll kill him. My father will kill him." Becca moves to the window, her eyes coursing with theories. "How'd you know?"

"What?"

"Henson. You said our last name and it came to you something fierce. How? If you know what happened to Dane you need to tell me, Emily. My family loves him. If you know where he is or if he's hurt—"

"He's planted on the south side of the driveway," I say softy. "His grave is but a few days old."

"No."

"I'm sorry."

"No!" she screams. "Say it isn't true. Tell me he isn't buried on that bastard's farm!"

I stand from the wastebasket. "His is but one of many graves on that farm. I've yet to find my husband's."

Emily tears from the room in a frenzy. "Janice!" Her cries fade as she briskly scurries away. "Janice, is that Dad pulling in the drive?"

I collapse into the chair behind me. I don't feel rejuvenated having confessed my secrets to Becca. I feel vile through association. I feel unsheltered.

***

"Child, your story is the stuff of nightmares. The sad thing is that story comes a dime-a-dozen in this neck of the woods," Earl declares. "How many?" he asks softly from the chair by the door.

"How many what?" I respond while sitting on the bed in the guestroom. Becca stands next to her father.

"How many bodies has that man put in the ground?"

"I'm not sure. Several, I imagine."

"Do you have names?"

"No," I whimper. "I'm sorry." The names I do have will stay tucked tight behind my lips to avoid any additional implication.

"That settles it. I knew that bastard was no good…rotten to the core. I didn't know he was capable of this bullshit." Earl stands from his chair. "Becca, round the boys up."

"What will you do?" I ask.

"We're going up the road. I'm bringing my boy home," he replies with a quake to his voice.

"What of Leroy—"

"He knew that boy was good as family round here. He knew this was coming." Earl opens the door to leave.

"Wait," I stammer. "If you are to take his life…please…please don't take his life before he tells you where my husband is buried."

My plea pauses his exit. "Emily," he chuckles softly, yet manically, "that man isn't dying tonight. And I promise you I'll get any questions you want answered…answered."

22.

"Kaleb, the door is stuck tight. It won't budge. Why would he lock us down here?"

With only the light of a single long-stem candle, I walk about the dank dungeon of a cellar. A pungent, sour aroma, like that of a stale wash, is all through the underground lair.

"Meyrick," Kaleb sobs, "this is misery. Why would they do this to us? We're not criminals."

Kaleb remains tucked in a weathered blanket in the center of the floor, from any of the living walls. Once more I ascend the cement steps to push forcefully on the door from beneath. My efforts are fruitless.

Candle in hand, I return to a bundled Kaleb. As I near him, his brow creases and nostrils flare. "Meyrick, something's wrong," he cries out—shaking his head."

"We've been in worse jams, boy. We'll be out of this—"

"Meyrick!" His shaking finger is pointing below my midriff. The dancing flame illuminates my soiled gown, drenched in a devastating burgundy along my thighs.

"No! Kaleb...oh no. The baby!" I crumple to the floor. Only now is the pain in my belly evident. "Kaleb...the baby..." I whimper, dragging myself through filth to reach him.

Within one another's arms, in complete squalor, we cradle each other as the cellar door flings open from above. So bright is the light it's nearly blinding as it floods the dank and smelly crypt.

"Hello down there!" The portly, drunken gentleman who stowed us down here only hours prior now hobbles

down the stairs. "Howdy-do," he exclaims chipperly. "It's a damper scene down here, ain't it?"

"We need help. Please," I beg from my husband's arms.

"Hush that shit, woman. You all is here for a purpose. Round here, everything has a purpose."

He squats to the two of us, dust dances in the sunlight behind him. If only Kaleb could run, we'd knock him away and make our getaway up those haggard steps.

"Damn, girl. You're just bleedin' like a stuck hog. I'll toss down some tissues for ya lady business—"

"Please," I interject. "You don't understand."

"Nah, bitch. You don't understand. I don't give a fuck about whatever you're down here crying about. I'm just here to trim the fat." He grins. His smile is as grotesque as the roaches scurrying about the creases of our confinements.

"Trim the fat?" I ask reluctantly.

"It all serves a purpose…and when it don't, it's gotta go. That there boy ain't nothin' more than another mouth to feed. Busted up leg. No good round here."

"What?" I gasp. "What are you planning to do?"

"I aim to do what any good farmer does when stock goes lame, put that shit down." He slaps his thighs and stands.

"No! You can't be…you cannot be serious. He'll heal. This isn't…you can't. This is lunacy." Kaleb squeezes me from behind.

"Little lady. Do I look like the kind of man what goes about my day foolin' around? Now if you little shits don't get all stupid, I'll give ya my word it'll be clean

and quick. But if you go to hootin' and hollerin' and acting ridiculous, I'll put a hurt on that boy they'll hear up in Alaska before I toss him in the ground."

"No," I cry. "Please. I'll do anything. Please, I'm begging you! Please!"

***

"Emily!" My eyelids fling open. "Emily, it's okay. You're okay," Becca says kindly while wiping my tears away.

"Oh, Becca!" Sitting forward in the bed, I readily accept the embrace Becca offers. "He's gone. He took him! He's gone!"

"Talk to me. I'm here. Tell me." Her soft words have me wanting to divulge the details—to purge the pain. There's no purging. I know this sorrow is in me physically forever.

"He was hurt," I whisper into her shoulder.

"Your husband?"

"Kaleb. His name was Kaleb. He was hurt and we were locked away in this awful place…this hole of a cellar." Hearing the words aloud is torturous and yet I continue. "He said he was lame and had to be put down…he dragged him away like he was nothing. He wasn't *nothing*. He was everything."

"What kind of a monster…and you? What of you?"

I cling to her tighter, ensuring my face is free of her view. "He left me there to bleed. I'm unsure how long—it all blended. I know it was dark when he collected me from the floor and toted me up the steps. He told me to wash it away in the bathroom…to wash the blood and muck…the remnants of my family away. And then he gave me a choice."

"A choice?"

"A choice," I mutter. "Stay. Eat, drink and sleep…become the woman of the house with *all* of her bestowed obligations. Or leave. Walk away."

"Emily, you—"

"I'm disgusting. I'm the foulest being breathing—"

"That was never a choice, Emily!" Becca declares as she holds me away, attempting to connect. "You would have died. You *were* dying, because of him. That wasn't a choice, ever."

"I should have walked into the darkness. I should have faded away that night," I sob.

"No, Emily—"

"I've been fading ever since!"

"You chose to live, Emily. Do *not* chastise yourself for choosing to survive." She squeezes me once more. "Your strength shows in your choice. You did what was necessary to keep breathing. That's a survivor."

"Oh, Becca…the things I've done. The things he made me do."

"The things he's done, sweet girl. Someday you'll see you're not the demon. I hope it's sooner rather than later because you've got a lot of life left in ya."

"If there is life left in me it's miniscule at best. I'm hollow and empty."

She smiles kindly while wiping my face. "If that's true, where are all these tears coming from?" Taking my hands in hers, she squares her shoulders. "We're going to find Kaleb. We're going to give him a proper resting place. You're going to thrive. You're going to get closure and you're going to bloom brighter than any flower on this property and you and I are going to be friends for years to come."

"Closure? I don't even know what that looks like or

where it begins—"

"It begins where he ends, Emily. My dad and his boys are at that hellhole right now. I assure you that answers are being sung beautifully. And when they get that bastard back here—"

"What? Here? Why on earth would they bring Leroy here?" Anxiety clutches my breath at the thought of seeing him again.

She offers my thigh a sisterly patting. "The spoon in my daddy's mouth wasn't always silver. He's had to work real hard to get this slice of heaven. Just because he walks in here, polished and gentleman-like, doesn't mean he won't get his hands good and dirty to defend what he's built. Daddy's got his hands dirty plenty of times…especially when it comes to protecting the folks he loves."

"I don't understand. What does that have to do with bringing Leroy here…to this place?"

Becca chuckles. "There's more than one farmstead around here with a body or two buried outback of a barn."

"I don't want to see him. I never want to see him again—"

"No, no, no. Come here, let me show you something." I'm led from the bed, to the end of the corridor. "You see past them trees? That big round-top?" She points out the window and well past the tree line.

"I do."

She only grins and nods.

"There? That's barbarism," I mumble.

"No, that's life. That's our life. That man will confess each and every one of his sins and then he'll be dispatched. No need for people like that in the world."

"So that's it then? He's gone…that easily."

"That easily. He's only a man, Emily. He's a cruel and worthless man and his actions have earned him this ending."

"When will they return?" I mutter.

"No clue. Depends on what they find…who they find."

It's inescapable. I close my eyes and his voice is there to violate my slumber. I open them and he's engrained into my reality. He is my reality. He's forever a part of me. How is one to heal from that?

I wonder how my brown-eyed assassin is taking to the marauding guests. Surely, they've fled the area for the woodlands. I wonder if my hosts will revoke my welcome once Leroy has disclosed each grisly detail— once he's painted me the vengeful murderess. I wonder if he'll plead for his life, or remain cold and unyielding in his final hours.

"Emily, don't waste your tears on trash like Leroy Ellis. That animal has a twisted sense of entitlement. His land and that shack of a house were tossed at him by his daddy. Everything he touches he assumes he can sour and make his own." She looks to me. "That is not you."

Even now, knowing his existence is in the midst of being eviscerated, his cruelty flutters about in my brain like a maimed butterfly on the sidewalk— *'Say it! Say it!'* "I am yours," I mutter, looking toward the round top barn.

"Come again, Emily?"

"Nothing. Do you mind if I go for a walk about the property? I need to refresh my lungs."

"I'm not sure, Emily. Dad should be back anytime and—"

"I won't go far, only the front yard…just to the trees there," I reply while pointing.

A few hesitant seconds later she nods. "Okay. But if you so much as hear a truck, just head on back inside. You don't need to witness anything that goes on past the trees," she states vacantly.

"Becca, does much take place out past the trees…in that round-top barn with the rusted roof?"

She turns, resting her back to the glass. "This is a beautiful place. There's plenty of beautiful people and families and homes. There's plenty of ugly too. Everything about that barn is ugly, but necessary."

"I don't understand."

"Emily, my daddy has been struggling for years…and not to keep this place afloat. He's had hell trying to keep the likes of people like Ricardo Ramirez and Alexander Hazleton at bay. Those names…those names you'll hear spat and cursed daily."

"Ricardo?" I say inquisitively.

"An awful human. A virus. He makes his living by dissembling others' dreams and leaving them defenseless with no means to escape."

"Please, Becca, explain to me exactly—"

"People come here to work. Some of them…most of them have no plan b, no other options. Some are lost in translation. They're cash-poor, some are even starving by the time they get here." Her gaze migrates to the ceiling. "Life can be hard here. The work is hard, the days are long and not everyone's dreams align with reality. Look at you, Emily. Pretty little thing like you…do you really think it's coincidence that you fell into the lap of Leroy Ellis?"

"No. Leroy told me of Ricardo. He told me of his dealings."

"Ricardo, Alexander…the area is spotted with a few smaller names but the real snakes in the grass…"

"And your father has been feuding with these people because they're monsters and he is not?"

"My father can only run this farm because of the hardworking employees that help him keep it operating. He is nothing like Ricardo. And yet every time someone makes it to this property, all shook up and offering tidbits of the saddest story your ears ever heard…it's those bastards at the center of it. They deal, trade, and discard these people as if they're property…less than property."

"Discard? What do you mean discard?"

"A man who can't work a field, be it a busted bone or some illness…he's nothing more than a loss of an investment to some folks…a bed that needs emptied so they can fill it with an able body. Ricardo can take a…twenty-something field-working boy who's laid up and sell him—"

"Sell him?" I exclaim.

"A reshuffling fee, for little of nothing. Farmers looking for the cheapest labor will scrape the bottom of the barrel…invest in Ricardo's goods in the hopes they'll return to the fields for pennies on the dollar once their ailments dissipate. Then there's you." She shakes her head. "When a pretty face like yours makes it to these parts…I hear the going rate's a bit higher."

"That's barbaric."

"And when there's no takers, lame hands just…disappear."

"Disappear?"

"Or my father, or someone else with the ability to be a human, finds them wandering around the backwoods after they've managed to get away."

"That's appalling. How could something so vile take place?"

"That, Emily, is why my father has been feuding with them. Leroy Ellis is nothing more than a metastatic process…a tiny cancer resulting from a much larger malignancy. The real problem in these parts is Ricardo Ramirez and Alexander Hazleton. Their operations have poisoned the area and the folks around here who aren't benefitting from them are too scared to retaliate. As long as they're breathing—"

"He's not," I sputter before processing what implications my disclosure may have. She turns to me, her gaze alive with inquisitiveness.

"Say what?"

The breath I draw is deep, as if I'm lakeside and seconds from plunging into the water. I exhale, yet no anxiety escapes past my lips. "I need to confess…I need to tell you something, Becca." My voice cracks—vision blurs as I prepare to divulge.

"Please do, Emily," she replies softly.

"He came to me, at the farmhouse. The man you call Ricardo came to me. I was confused as to what he wanted or if he wanted…I only knew he was cold and his eyes were the cruelest I'd seen."

"Emily, what happened?"

"I led him away from the house and to the barns." Tears fall to the floor below. Fat and full, they slap against the marble. "There, in the barns, he ordered me to undress…to undress as he was, as a means of payment."

"Emily, did he—"

"I was confused. I'm unsure of the debt he was speaking of."

"Oh, sweetheart."

She inches closer but her advancement has me shying away. The truth is blazing to leave my mouth and can't be quelled under an embrace. She must know. "There was a mallet…it happened so quickly."

Seconds pass in stillness and when I gather the courage to glance her in the eyes, I'm taken aback to find her silently rejoicing. Her grin can't be corralled as she cautiously steps to me.

"Emily," she chokes. "Are you telling me you killed that sick bastard before he man-handled you?"

I nod once and am instantly taken in her arms. "That's the most beautiful thing I've heard in years," she says softly into my ear. "You are one hell of a woman…one hell of a human!"

As we decouple, both wiping our faces, I find I'm comfortably relieved to have disclosed my deed. Her reaction is unexpected yet uplifting. "Your father…will he be angry with what I've done? I've been so horrified of him finding out the truth before I can explain."

"Heavens no!" Her enthusiasm fills the corridor. "My father will be delighted to hear Ricardo is dead. He'll be tickled pink to learn you killed the bastard while defending yourself."

A sense of reprieving euphoria has me grinning too. "Well then. I'm certainly glad that's over with."

"Emily, this is good. This is a great thing! Ricardo's evil flowed down. With him gone, it's only a matter of time before it will dissipate. You cut the head off the snake, girl! I can't wait until my dad hears about this."

Visions of other acts of violence and farmyard secrets hinder me from completely enjoying this moment with Becca. I'm certain that nothing spewed from Leroy's mouth will be deemed credible but the thought of his disclosure has me writhing inside. The off-chance that Anna and Q are discovered, what of them? Will they join me here in this haven for broken things? Will Anna implicate herself in the murder of their beloved Dane? Certainly not. Anna and Q are far too clever and self-preservation is understandably their top priority.

"I think I'll join you."

"I beg your pardon?" I reply.

"On your walk. I can introduce you to the groundskeeper, show you the property, and let you look around without feeling like you're trespassing."

"Oh. That's kind. To be completely honest it isn't really a walk I desire at all. I only want to sit beneath the trees, just there," I point. "I'd like to be with my thoughts and hear the birds…feel the wind move around me."

"I totally get it. Go on. I'll start us some tea so it's ready when you get back. We've got plenty to celebrate today, Emily!"

The stroll to the woods is an odd one. Typically, the trees reach out to me—their branches ready to wrap me in an organic safety. The kinship I felt with the woodlands surrounding my community and Leroy's farmstead was an immense source of comfort. One vast, enigmatic friend, alive and teeming. Here, as I approach, the trees do not welcome. They seem cold and unhospitable. With each step in their direction, I feel as though I'm inching further from safety. Still, I meander, and when I've reached the tree line I gawk about cautiously before seating myself in the plush grass.

The Henson home is close enough I can easily identify the individual flowers within the wooden window boxes, yet it feels impossibly distant.

Before, I'd spend my daily hour doing just what I am now, sitting beneath the luscious canopy and listening to the clamorous chatter of countless dwellers. Now, however, I'm uneasy and contemplating returning after just a few brief minutes.

Perhaps it isn't the trees or the woodlands here at all, but rather the entirety of the ongoing situation. Sealing my eyelids, clutching the grass beneath me, I take in nature's tranquility.

No sooner has the tension in my shoulders eased, carried off on a mild breeze, and I'm hearing a rustling from just within the woods. My eyes snap open, peering through the tree trunks for encroachers.

"Emily," the trees whisper. "This is you?"

"Who is there?" I respond immediately as I find my footing.

"Emily." Several meters within the vegetation I see her, Anna's beautiful face and a bashful Q standing just behind her. Their dewy, fresh faces are a welcome sight.

"Oh, my goodness!" Into the trees I dart, ducking under branches and maneuvering around trunks and vines until I'm with them once more. "How is this possible? How are you here?"

"What? Emily, we are here for you," Anna replies.

"But Leroy…what happened after I ran? I was so

worried."

She passively plucks a few twigs from my clothing. "No need for worry, my beauty. You were there. You saw his injury. He's going nowhere."

"How did you manage to escape?" I enquire forcefully.

She studies my expression a moment or two before laughing hardily from her belly. "Manage to escape? This is too funny, Emily. I crushed his crusty foot with a hammer and left him crying like a toddler. We walked away and enjoyed the sunrise. This is how we managed to escape."

"And you've been here, just roving about the wood? You must be famished and completely exhausted."

My concern elicits an additional chuckle. "Oh, sweet Emily. Even at your lowest you're concerned for others. Oh, so sweet."

"I've been safe here. I have learned things." I rest my hand on her shoulder. "Anna, the man on the farm…on the yard, he came from this place. He was a good man."

My hand is abrasively shrugged away. "All men are good or bad, depending on who you are asking. They all toss their money and morals away for pretty faces…they all bleed, and die if the blade goes deep enough. They're flies. All the same."

"Anna—"

"Ssshhh. Such a pretty mouth, such stupid words, and I don't want to hear them."

"Anna, why have you come here? To be crass and cruel?"

"We are here for you. You know this."

"As we speak, there are men scouring Leroy's farm

for answers. They'll collect those answers as well as Leroy and bring them here. He will tell them of his sins…as well as mine."

"And you will tell your new friends of the lies he speaks. Nothing but lies from his rotten mouth," she grumbles passively.

"I know his end is near, yet I fear what may come before it—"

"Fear?" Anna repeats. "What fear should come of this? You know how this ends—"

"Do *not* tell me that again!" I exclaim. "I know nothing."

She steps from me. Beneath the dense and swaying limbs, it is quite warm and yet I'm shivering at her stare.

"Emily!" Becca calls from the house as the sound of a vehicle engine roars about the area.

"You better run along. You are being called," Anna says softly.

"I'll try to bring you provisions this evening, just stay out of sight."

My offer is disregarded as I'm shooed away like a pest.

"Emily!" I hear once more as I exit the trees. I see her waiting for my return as I make my way toward the home hastily. She ushers me in the backdoor with an ill-concealed grin, as if she's expecting a divine guest, not a sinister entourage. "Come inside, girl. I've made us some tea. It sounds like the boys are back."

At the table, I watch her sip with shaking hands and buzzing eyes. Each swallow is loud with tension in the still room.

"Becca, will he suffer greatly?"

My question seems to have her squirming in her chair. "Did…did you suffer greatly, Emily? Have others suffered because of him?"

"You're answering a question with a question. I'm going to assume that means yes."

"I don't know, Emily. I haven't stuck my nose in my father's messy business, and for good reason. I don't wanna know the gritty details."

"The secrets tucked in the trees," I mutter into my cup.

A door opens behind me, Illuminating Becca's face as light floods the dark room. "Hey Daddio," she says guardedly. "How are things?"

"Beautiful. Just beautiful."

My chest pounds uncomfortably as Earl removes his boots and steps into the dining room. "We found Dane. Found a couple of Ricardo's boys too…what was left of them. That stench could gag a skunk. Tossed the dirt back and left that trash where we found it."

"And Dane? Did you bring him home?" Becca asks.

"Oh yes. Dane will be laid to rest here," he asserts as he joins us at the table. "That bastard Leroy sang like bird. Confessed before I had to unlock my toolbox."

Leroy's confession may have vindicated me, yet the initial relief is overcome by an anxious idea that Leroy will be disposed of prior to disclosing my husband's resting place. "And Kaleb? What of Kaleb?" I interject.

"Who?" Earl replies as he removes his ballcap and tosses it on the table.

"My husband. I must know where my husband is buried," I state frantically.

"Okay, okay," he responds calmly. "Leroy ain't in the ground yet. I told you I'd find your husband and I will."

23.

The evening comes and is anything but soothing. It moves in like predators surrounding their dying dinner. My thoughts gnaw and scratch about in my skull as I pace the corridor. A pale, violet sky, calm and windless, blankets the sinister trees while they vigilantly guard their play-home of obscurities beneath the rusted tin-roof. I wonder what obscurities brew there this evening.

With each stride, the length of the hallway, the sky, and my thoughts darken a touch more. Every inch of my being is electrified in a tainted energy—a vitality stemming from fear, like children running from an angry wasp colony in a forest after tormenting their hive.

The night takes the sky and I am alone by choice. I slide down the wall until my backside meets the cold floor and my gaze settles on a vast, black nothing through the windows. The deconstruction of Leroy Ellis is something I've long craved—fantasized over, even. Now, as it unfolds within running distance, I find the idea of it unsettling—and this perplexes me.

My head to the wall, my veins coursing with a negative toxicity, I find it odd that closing my eyes comes so easily even with my chest hammering away.

The corridor is silent, the only sound is the pulse in my ears—steady and thunderous. I fade into it…

It has been less than a week and I'm fearful of Kaleb's smile fading from my mind. Surely something so beautiful will be ever etched on my memory like an epitaph in stone. I close my eyes and he's there, grinning. I haven't a photograph to cherish, only my reminiscence.

We were established in our bond and it isn't something that can be wiped away like blemishes from glass. Yet, there is a lingering fear that his face will drift from me, and I will be left in this dreadful place with a headful of dreadful thoughts.

Leroy watches me the way a starved hound might watch an empty bowl. He's a peculiar gentleman, and if there's a single redeeming quality floating about his atrocious being, it is lost to the fact he took my husband from me.

The men of my community move and respond a certain way. When in groups, they are schools of fish, shifting predictably and claustrophobically close to one another. When alone, their faux smiles and canned conversations are as humdrum as one of Father's post-sermon-sermons. Kaleb was his own man...but Leroy is as well.

Leroy is the form of ugly that demands a second glance yet begs one's gaze be diverted. He roars through this scrapheap of a house, belligerent and unruly of a morning. He pays no mind to the lady in the home as his nudity is on full display—in and out of the rooms as he yells about, searching for tools and articles of clothing.

Last night he required my presence in his bedroom. On his lumpy and damp mattress, I laid utterly motionless until his monstrous snores filled the room. I fear I may be required to return, night after night, and that more than lying still will be required.

I have never detested something more. I wish death on him. He left the home today. My week has been spent in mourning and filth. Each room of the home now resembles a room of a home rather than a collection of rubbish. I long to leave this decrepit shack. I wish to run from here and lie atop my husband's gravesite and fade into him—I want to rot with him. He could be anywhere in the forsaken area...dappled in broken dreams and desolate farms.

The trees offer the only sense of comfort here. They encompass this home and wave to me through the milky windows. Today I'll join them. I'm unsure of my plans afterwards. I know only that I wish to walk in the trees and water them with my tears. I wish to mourn my husband without a dishrag in my grasp and a cruel word in my ear.

The mouth of the woodlands is opened and welcoming. Under their cradling branches, I crumple and cry on the forest floor. My face to the earth, I wail and pay no mind to what I may be disturbing. I inhale the stagnant air—perfumed with decaying leaves and dank soil. Each hair on my forearms stands erect as the cries of something wild tear through the branches.

As I peer past a crumbling log, I catch a glimpse of something brown scampering about within the cover of a large spruce. From the commotion I witness a tiny blue object fall from the treetops to the forest floor. It's dashed against the rocks and branches below, spilling its contents—an egg.

The calls grow louder as I arise to witness the spectacle. Two gorgeous ravens seek revenge on this nest-robbing squirrel and I find I'm most enchanted by the idea of retribution.

I grin as the squirrel squirms and twists about in the air, falling to the ground and landing harshly atop pointed stones. I completely lack empathy as it is dispatched in a manner most brutal just before me.

Cold, cunning, and aggressively loyal, I long to solicit their violence. I long to beckon the ravens and unleash their ferocity on him. Oh, to watch from afar as he is dismembered pitilessly and held accountable for my suffering. To return the agony he bestowed on me when he took my beloved husband. I long to beckon them. I long to beckon the ravens...

I awake in a panic, my back to the wall as I glance about the corridor for onlookers, either feathered or not. A dark dread cuts short my inhalation as I contemplate an awful possibility. "He won't tell them. They'll end him tonight and I'll never know where my husband is buried," I mumble.

Scrambling sloppily atop the slick marble river, I find my footing while searching for my courage. "Move."

I leave the corridor and rush through the backdoor, completely unsure of my intentions. The night's air is warm and opaque with the songs of the creatures in the trees. Barefoot and uncertain, I race from the light of the front yard and to the woodland. I don't fear what waits there—glowing eyes or growling from the shadows. I fear what lingers beneath the tin roof, what I might witness once I'm there.

Sharp things mean to slow me. They prod and pierce my feet as I move through the unfamiliar forest. Weaving through the trees meticulously, I finally reach a clearing and the guarded barn. Lit only by a pale, yellow moon glow, the sight of the monstrous round-top halts me in my tracks. Rust adorns its rippled tin-roof, extending down the sides and to the ground as if it's bleeding out.

Slowly, I advance toward the barn from the thicket. With each footstep, the yearning to turn and flee intensifies. The only windows are blacker than the darkest pieces of the sky above me. The door is a cold-looking metal and is closed. There are no signs of life here other than the vivacity from the trees and sky. Perhaps I'm too late. Perhaps my nightmares have been dismantled and have been put away for the earth to digest. I may never know of my husband's resting place…or perhaps they pried that piece of information from Leroy in some gruesome fashion?

Stepping backwards and away from the barn's front door seems to lesson my angst. An additional step and I'm on the verge of darting back to the trees…but then, through the back windows, there is light. Miniscule bits of light peek through and I realize the glass has been painted black. There may be life within this rusted tin box of a building.

Inching forward, I reach the metal door to find it's as cold and unwelcoming as I'd imagined. Light pierces the night as I push and it opens slowly. My face to the door, I slide in gradually. The buzzing, white glow of the lights above is almost blinding. I initially see only a large vacant building with a dirt floor and tables aligning the walls—cluttered with tools. Long and grand, the vacant building darkens at the opposing end. Near the other end positioned centrally within the shadows, is lump in a chair.

"Le…Leroy?" I mutter as I tread toward the back of the building. Each sliding step agitates the floor and has the dust dancing in the fading light as I approach this confined figure. "Is that you?"

It is him, all that remains. Bound, broken and

bloodied in a shabby wooden chair, Leroy makes no movement. So battered is his face that he is almost unidentifiable.

Inching closer to this lifeless man, I find the emotional rift within me more troubling than the visual in the chair. The urge to strike him, even now—to pummel his streaked and swollen face, surges in me. It balls my fists and grits my teeth. And yet my eyes well with tears. My knees tremble and I'm perplexed at the compulsion to fall to them, to wail for this fiend who's anguished my existence. I loathe the inability to escape this odd empathy and even sense of mourning for him. "Godspeed, Leroy Ellis," I whisper before turning somberly.

"Meyrick?" I hear him hack out.

The initial relief to find him breathing is oppressed by repulsion at myself for being relieved. "Leroy?"

"Help me...please help me, Meyrick," he pleads softly while glancing about through engorged plums for eyes.

"How? And why would I help you, Leroy?"

He crumbles before me. His cries are silent, yet the tears seep and trickle down his face. "I'm sorry." His raspy, pathetic whisper is nearly inaudible.

"Leroy—"

"Run me through, Meyrick. Please."

"What? Leroy, I'm not here to—"

"The things they said they's gonna do to me," he sobs. "Ungodly things. Things I won't repeat for a lady shouldn't hear 'em. Please, don't leave me here to die like that. Please run me through."

My throat tightens as if a fist is clenching it from the inside. "Leroy, I can't do that."

"Please, Meyrick. You owe me nothin'. It's probably the ending you thought most fitting but I know you's a good person. I know you are. Please…don't no one deserve to die that way. I'm beggin' ya."

"Leroy…where is he? Tell me," I ask as I kneel to him.

"Earl? I got no clue. That's why you gotta do this quick with a screwdriver or—"

"No," I interject. "Where is my husband buried? I need to know before I do anything."

"Meyrick…dammit."

"Tell me, or I'm leaving."

My question quells his movement. Slowly, he diverts his hindered gaze. "He ain't."

"Leroy, if I'm going to help you, I need to know," I repeat as I position myself on my knees before him.

"He ain't buried, Meyrick," he says lowly. "At least not to my knowledge."

"You didn't bury him? You just left him to—"

"I told you he had a choice," he snaps, looking at me once more. "That day…that morning I took that ol' boy out. He was just a beggin' and cryin'." Leroy pauses, as if reflecting. "I ain't never seen a man get on like that. Got to me more than it shoulda. Truth be told, the boy hadn't done me no harm. So, I gave him a choice."

"What choice?" I demand.

"I told him I'd tuck my blade away. I'd pick him up out that field, take him to the trade barn and leave him to his own devices." He looks to me once more, our stares locking. "In exchange for you. His life for you. Told him if he came back round, I'd kill the both of ya."

"He's alive?" I cry out shakenly.

"Was when I dumped him. No clue how he faired with that busted leg."

I stand, in shock. "You let me believe this entire time…I've been in mourning this entire time, and he's alive?"

"I couldn't do it, Meyrick. He weren't but a boy on the ground beggin' me. If I'd told you, you'd a done took off after him."

"Leroy! We had a life! We are people…we hurt."

"Likewise!" he shouts. "I'm sorry. Meyrick, them men could be back any minute. I ain't askin' you to forgive me. I'm askin' you to run me through so them bastards don't gut me like a damn hog! Please!"

Glancing about the dusty tables, my mind encumbered with what I've just learned, I spy a serrated blade and retrieve it. As I move to his binds, he appears nearly taken aback.

"What are you doin'?"

"Giving you a choice, Leroy. Setting you free. I hope you choose to be better."

"Meyrick…I can't walk on this busted foot—"

"Could Kaleb walk when he was set free? Hobble…crawl, do what you must, but go to the trees. Leave this place and don't come back."

He nods—his grin and the majority of his expression is hindered by inflammation. I maneuver around him and just as the blade meets the binds my ears catch the sound of metal-door opening.

"Meyrick, whatchu waitin' on? I gotta get."

"Silence, Leroy. We're not alone," I whisper as I slink around to see who approaches.

"What? Meyrick—"

"Be quiet!" I snap.

They leisurely advance into the shadowed area of the barn…Anna and Q.

"Why are you here?"

Anna smiles slyly as she meanders nearer, her meek partner trailing just behind. "You know how this ends, my beauty," she replies.

"Meyrick, who the fuck—"

"Silence, Leroy!" I yell.

"Hand me the weapon, Emily," she says. Her smoky demand is accompanied with an open hand, prompting me to hand over the blade.

"Whatever for?"

"You know. It is time. It ends tonight…now."

"No," I reply, shaking my head and stepping from her. "No, no that isn't what I've chosen to do. Anna, you have a family to concern yourself with. You should leave here now."

Her hands rest atop her taut belly, as does her gaze. "Family?" she sneers. "A baby no more."

"What?" I exclaim. "Anna, how? When? I'm so sorry, I didn't know—"

"You always knew, my beauty. You know. Now give me the weapon."

I tuck the blade behind me as she moves closer. "Anna, this is not what I choose. I choose forgiveness."

She smiles and advances, softly cradling me in an embrace. I'm comforted by the way her chin fits contently on my shoulder, her breath soft and warm on my ear. Her hands slide over my forearms and I offer no resistance as she retrieves the blade from my grasp. "We choose vengeance," she whispers just prior to our decoupling.

Her eyes have never been darker. There's an

intensity in them that assures me her intentions are secure.

"Meyrick," Leroy barks. "What in god's name is going on?"

"I'm so sorry, Leroy," I reply as Anna and Q position themselves on either side of their confined victim.

"Sorry for what? What the fuck is goin' on?" he cries out, his voice strained in fear.

"We choose vengeance," Anna replies. "We choose vengeance."

With one hand resting atop his sweating, quivering head, the other aligns the blade with his puffy left eye. His screams fill the barn as Anna drives the blade into his eye socket.

His wailing and thrashing about, as well as the copious amount of blood produced by the action, have me turning from the barbaric scene and falling to my knees. "Anna! Enough! You have your vengeance!" I scream out.

His agony intensifies, his screams are horrific. The sounds produced as the blade does its damage have me gagging and longing to drive my fingers into my ears. "Anna, please! Stop! Enough!"

Several seconds, perhaps minutes, pass and his screams are reduced to gurgling. It is only now I notice we have been joined by onlookers. Earl and other men watch from several feet away near the front of the barn. Their expressions are eclectic—some horrified, others amused, but my focus has settled on Earl's devious grin as he watches intently the butchering taking place just behind me. The evil dancing in his eyes is as sinister as any evil that came from Leroy—branding it as revenge doesn't make it justifiable.

It appears Leroy's pathetic gasps have been quelled. The barn is perfumed in a dreadful reek, reminiscent of childhood days when my father and uncle would butcher livestock in our barn. I arise and gather the courage to look upon what they have reduced him to. I lose my breath completely as I do—falling back to the dusty floor.

Leroy's face has been pierced relentlessly. His eyes have been plucked and stabbed away. The bloated and hairy belly I've long despised is now split and purging pink, bloody coils onto the dirty floor beneath. He breathes no more. He is gone.

"Monsters," I stammer. "You are both monsters. You *are all* monsters!"

"Sightless and hollow," Anna replies excitedly as she approaches with a winded grin.

"What?"

"Sightless and hollow. This is how it ends. You knew how it would end…we have been here before, my beauty."

I press my hands to either side of my head. "I've never…I don't understand. Anna, you're an awful human being. I despise you—"

"You beckoned me," she interjects with a giggle. "A walk in the woods…two beautiful birds…and an ugly, fat rodent."

"How? I've never told you that—"

"So sad, your face, seeing that beautiful blue shell, shattered on rocks." She once again glances toward her stomach and pats it. "You know this story. You were so sad to see the ravens go."

"Anna, I need you to tell me what is happening."

"Sightless and hollow. You beckoned the ravens. You beckoned us and we have been here for you. We have always been here for you, my beauty."

"Emily," Earl's voice shakes me from behind.

"You!" I scream out as I rage toward him. "How could you let them! You stood there smiling!"

His expression twinges in confusion as he crosses his arms. "Emily, what would you have had me do? We were set on lettin' this bastard slither outta here but I know there's a bit of history there and I wasn't about to jump in the middle of that mess when you had that blade in your hand."

"My hand? Blade in my hand?" I exclaim. "You could have stopped the two of them. I didn't want this. You could have stopped them!" I shriek out.

"Them? What do you mean, them? Emily, there ain't no one here but us…and you."

His words are senseless, yet they have me looking about the barn behind me. "No, you saw them…they're…gone. They've left!" I cry out.

"Who? Who has left?" Earl demands as he levels his gaze with mine.

"Anna and Q, I tell you! You saw them! The people you watched butcher that helpless man, tied in that chair!"

He smiles—a smile that assures me he's deeply concerned. "Emily…I only saw you, wielding a knife."

"Lies!"

"Then why are you soaked in blood?"

Shaking, I glance downward to find my garments saturated in thick, sticky crimson. "No. Oh, god no."

"And why are you holding the blade?"

My trembling hand releases the bloody, jagged knife

from my grasp as my psyche disintegrates. "No. No, no, no, no. They weren't here? They were never? Oh no…oh no. How could that be? They were here! They had to be…" I mumble as I pace, my palms pressed to my face.

"Hey," Earl snaps sternly as he halts my stride and rests his hands atop my shoulders. "They were here, it was just different. They were here in a different way…and that's okay."

He catches me as I topple into him, wailing. My mind's conjuring of an occasional winged fiend or glistening feather was a manageable encumbrance. Even entertaining the possibility of my visitors being anything but guests of a physical form is maddening.

In Earl's arms, a rapid reflection on my time with Anna and Q has my knees buckling beneath me. If my guests were truly fabricated products of my ailing mind, *I am the monster*. I am the murderer. If Anna's hand never grasped the blade to take a life, then the blood is on my hands, every last drop. The idea is inconceivable. I dined and conspired with them. I shared my dreams and fears with her. How could they be anything less than my unfortunate guests in the smallest of the barns?

"Are you okay, dear?" Earl asks while cradling me. "Are they…still here?"

I lift my head from his broad chest to glance about the barn once more. There are only confused farmhands and the carnage displayed behind us—eyeless and unseamed—*sightless and hollow*. "No," I mutter.

"Who were they?" he asks politely.

As I bury my face into his shirt, I attempt to formulate an answer that might make sense to the both of us. "I think…I believe they were the ravens. I believe I beckoned them."

My answer has him gripping me tighter in his arms. "Okay," he replies softly.

"I'm not well, Earl," I whisper into his chest.

"It's okay, Emily."

"I'm not well."

24.

Winter has once again taken the land. He's shed the trees—plucked each one nude. Bitter and violent, the wind aches to invade this drafty home. It slams against the windows, rattling the panes and howls hauntingly down the chimney to animate the flames consuming the logs.

Stripped. Exposed. The season has taken the plush, green blankets and left nothing but icy accountability.

In the sitting room, I glance through the frosty window. Even indoors, my breath is visible if I wander too far from the flames. A knocking on the kitchen door requires that I do just that. Given the hour and horrendous conditions, I've no choice but to question the authenticity of the visitor.

With an afghan draped about my shoulders, I meander through the frigid home, over the atrocious green linoleum and to the door to find a grinning Becca peering in. She and Earl are typically the only guests who travel the one-way road to this rundown domicile. They bring provisions and kind words…companionship. This evening, however, as the sun loses her battle so early and the hostile winds long to work their way within and drive away any warmth from the home, I wish only to be alone.

"Come in, you fool," I usher Becca in and immediately motion her to the sitting room and the fireplace.

"Emily," she exclaims. "Come home with me. It's too cold. It hasn't been this cold in decades."

"I can't. You know I can't," I mutter as I tread to the flames.

"You've punished yourself long enough. This is silly. Come home with me. We want you there."

We sit on the divan, the same divan I've cried myself to sleep on many a night. "This isn't punishment, Becca. This is how it must be. This is how I want it…it's my choice."

"It's a stupid choice," she snaps. "You're still staying here, of all places, here? Your room at our house is turned down. I'll draw you a bath and make some tea. Let's play cards all night and eat popcorn…or hell, I don't know. Come home with me."

"That sounds beautiful. It truly does. What happens when they return, Becca? What happens when my imagination takes up a blade and begins wielding it once more? I'm not well, and therefore not safe. This is best…and it is my choice," I state assertively while gazing into the blaze.

"Have they?" she asks scornfully.

"I beg your pardon?"

"Have they returned?"

"No. They have not," I whisper. Talking of them or even thinking of them seems to place me in a state of unrest. Although I have not seen or heard my murderous Anna since the night she blinded and spilled poor Leroy, I am left to question my sanity each time I spy a curious raven lurking about the property or flying overhead. I've learned to ignore the birds and pay no thought to their legitimacy.

"Then it's settled. Let's go, the truck's toasty-warm."

"Goodbye, Becca."

We sit in silence a few seconds more. Perhaps she would argue if previous arguments hadn't been fruitless. Her gloved hand rests atop my knee, patting me gently.

"Goodbye, Em."

The sound of her truck's engine is drowned in the wind's ferociousness as she leaves me to the cold

I curl up beneath the afghans and quilts, hoping the night is a swift one and my dreams are gentle.

Blood leaves the cut on my palm at a steady flow. Three bright-red streams adorn my ring, middle and index finger like a painted trident. I watch it hypnotically paint the broken whiskey glass in the sink. The pain is relieving, it masks the ache of the psyche momentarily.

Nearly one month has passed since my arrival to this dingy place. This evening I feel filthier than the rag in my hand and more broken than the bloody glass in the sink. When he took Kaleb from me, I thought he'd taken everything...that he could take no more. I was wrong.

The sun is setting. I have come to dread this hour. His engine roars from down the road—nearly clockwork. I remain stationary as he barrels through the door, cursing and perfuming the kitchen with the stench of the field.

"Where's my plate?" he calls from the bathroom through the open doorway—the sound of his urine streaming into the toilet bowl resounds noisily.

"Soon," I reply, driving my thumb into my bleeding wound.

"Whatchu mean, soon?" Mere seconds later and he's at my side investigating my injury. "Damn you! That there is my good glass, Meyrick!"

"My apologies, Leroy. I was attempting to clean it...and have your drink prepared for your arrival."

"Well, how'd that work out for ya? Dammit! Where's my whiskey, Meyrick?" he shouts *belligerently.*

"Emily," I respond softly as I motion toward the bottle on the kitchen table.

"Nah...he was a hollerin' for Meyrick. I know what your name is."

"Please. I prefer Emily."

"And I prefer a clean house, a warm plate, and woman to love on. Now shut that yap and get my plate. You bleed enough as it is."

He pours his whiskey as I contemplate running my wrist along the broken glass and draining my essence into the grimy, rusty drain. "When will you tell me?"

"Are you still talkin', woman?"

"Please. Where is he?" I ask with my back still to Leroy.

The room falls silent for several seconds. When the sound of his clunking boots makes their way across the floor to me, I know something dreadful is coming. "It's just about time for you to learn your place!"

"No!" I awake to darkness. In a defensive manner, I cover my face with my hands and flail my feet. In these brief moments, as the reality floods into me and washes his physical threat away, I love Anna for what she did. Sitting forward, winded, I take comfort in knowing Leroy is not here...he isn't coming back, and the world will never hurt me more than it already has.

Dying embers give a red glare from the fireplace, but very little heat. Logs are added.

There's something hypnotic in the way the flames devour all they touch. Watching the fireplace seems to shift my thoughts from the desperation surrounding my existence.

The pipes in the kitchen sputter and grumble and spit when I attempt to prepare tea. They're frozen—the world feels frozen.

The night gives way to dawn. Pale, blue light graces the sitting room as I stand and stretch the stagnancy from my bones. I don't long for this…to deteriorate with this wretched home. I'm intrigued by thoughts of the future. Visions of a small garden and a hardbound-book on a stand are pleasing. A part of me believes my mind is mending, that this dwelling is mending now that the poisonous thorn has been carved away. What does one do with a mending mind?

The winds have ceased. A light snow has dusted the area, it shimmers in the rising sun. Glancing about the home, frigid yet tidy, I find no tasks to help me feel productive. Perhaps I'll dust once more, as I did yesterday. The humming of a vehicle's engine disrupts my plans and sours my mood immediately. Stumbling to the window, I'm irate to see the Henson truck approaching, yet again. "Damn you, Becca…"

In the bathroom I ensure I'm somewhat presentable—my hair and face aren't a fright, and then make my way irritably to the kitchen to wait. It is several minutes before she appears, bundled and frantic-looking as she scurries up the steps.

"Becca," I exclaim. "What do you need?"

Her eyes—they tell me something has happened. It could be incredibly devastating or something wonderful. Regardless, I'm too cross to concern much myself initially.

"Come with me, Emily," she sputters.

"I told you why I can't. I wish you'd respect that I

wish to be left alone—"

"It's different today. Everything is different today." Her voice gives and tears flow.

I offer no resistance, only a curious nod as I close the door behind me and make my way to the vehicle. No words are spoken during the short journey. She holds my hand as she weeps and drives down the icy road through the gray. Several scenarios play out in my mind. I find myself questioning the health of her father, perhaps even her health.

I've visited the Henson estate twice since Leroy's dispatching. Both times were at the insistence of Becca and both times had me longing to leave before my seat was warm beneath me. I wish only to be alone.

The home comes into view through the trees as I turn to her. "Please, Becca, what is this regarding? Clearly, you're upset. Is your father well?"

"He's well," she mutters. "He just got home about two hours ago," she continues as the truck comes to a halt in front of the house.

"I see. Are you quarreling? Please, tell me why you've brought me here. I'm not fond of guessing—"

"The trade barns…Dad caught wind of some talk at the trade barns yesterday."

"Some talk?"

"Your name…specifically," she replies as the vehicle hums and shakes.

"Am I in some sort of trouble, Becca?"

"No." She shakes her head as a grin etches across her face. "Friendly talk."

"I have no friends…you and your father…imaginary things."

"Tell that to her," Becca says as she points toward

the corridor.

Through the glass, it's morning glare, is a ghostly vision of a girl I once knew—an image from my past. "No. No, that can't be. That isn't…is she really…?"

"I promise ya she's just as much here as you or I."

Opening the door, I slide from the vehicle, ensuring not to take my gaze from her, my beautiful Jennet. As I move to the home, she's moving to the backdoor of the house and my heart has never raced more wildly.

It's all I can do to breathe as she races through the door and I cannot have her in my arms fast enough. We collide and fall to the icy ground, sobbing in a trembling embrace. I don't know what words will spill from her mouth but I know now my future. Be it a day or years to come, my existence and hers will be vigorously intertwined. She is my family and childhood best friend, and I will never forsake this feeling, having her in my arms.

"Meyrick!" she cries out. "I thought…I thought I'd never…"

We separate just enough to see one another as we corral our emotions. "How, Jennet? How are you here now?"

"I've found you," she whispers.

"How is it you're here?"

Her smile glistens in the morning sun and steady stream of tears. "Meyrick, so much happened after you left. So much."

"Jennet—"

"Seven girls total," she stammers. "Seven, came forward after you rescued Kaleb and fled. They spoke of the ungodly things my uncle did to them." She grins as the words leave her mouth, as if she's speaking of something joyful.

"That bastard…they're all bastards. What of the girls? How did you escape—"

"No, Meyrick, I left on my own accord. I left to find you, with the blessing of the Community. You're not a criminal. You're a hero."

"What?" I gasp.

"Your actions opened so many eyes. Your courage spread like fire. You gave those girls the strength they needed to come forward…you gave me the strength I needed to speak my truth."

"They believed you? And forgave you?"

"Yes, every word. I was defending myself. There is nothing to forgive. Meyrick, your father cries daily for you."

"My father can drown in those tears," I reply abrasively.

"Meyrick, because of you, the reeds are no more. Had you not taken Kaleb that night, the Community would have punished an innocent man. He likely would have died."

I take her hands in mine and inhale deeply. "You don't know, do you?"

"Know what?" she asks concernedly.

"I'm afraid I am a widow, Jennet." We sit in silence. Her expression twitches as she constructs her response.

"Meyrick." She smiles. "I didn't travel alone."

Second by second, I feel my pulse amplifying within my throat. "Jen…Jennet?"

"Come inside with me."

"No!" I cry out. "Is this real? Are you here and saying this?"

"Yes." She chuckles. "Come."

Hand-in-hand we arise from the icy ground and walk through the door of the home with Becca trailing behind. With each step I feel as though my knees may buckle and I may crash. Through the corridor and to the sitting room, we are met with a grinning Earl. He says nothing, but kisses my forehead before leaving.

Seated near the fire is a sight more beautiful than any poem or painting could capture. My husband has officially returned to me from the dead.

"Meyrick!" he shouts as he attempts to stand. He hobbles and walks with a lean, severely favoring one foot over the other.

By the time I reach him, he's too emotional to speak. His cries fill the sitting room and he shakes violently within my embrace. It is now that I am completely convinced this is a cruel fiction concocted while sleeping.

His scent, the way he melts into me…it's all too much. "Tell me this isn't a dream. Are you truly here with me?" I say aloud.

"Forgive me!" he cries loudly into my ear. "Please forgive me!"

"What?"

"I'm sorry! I'm so sorry—"

"No, no, no." With his face in my hands I kiss him repeatedly, and still it isn't enough.

"I left. I left you!"

Even now, as he fractures before me—a slobbering, teary mess, I can't help but grin. "You had no choice."

"I'm weak!"

"As am I."

"My leg, Meyrick, I'm broken."

"As am I, as are we all. I have never loved anything

more than you. There was no greater gift than time left with you and now you are here. How is it that you are here?"

Trembling, he squeezes me tightly. "You could forgive me? Even now?"

In the arms of this quivering, damaged human, I feel a sense of safety resurrecting. "You are my husband, Kaleb. There is nothing to forgive."

We are joined by Jennet for a sobbing yet joyful reunification. My buzzing mind is nearly incapable of digesting the event. Maddened with euphoria, I grin and cry and kiss instantaneously.

As we separate, my life's pieces finally falling within my grasp, I assure one issue is addressed immediately. "I can't go back. I won't go back...ever."

Kaleb nods, wiping his face. "We'll go somewhere. There are always places looking for help," he states as he glances at his foot unsurely.

"Emily," from the doorway, Becca interjects. "Breakfast will be ready soon. Please, stay."

"Yes," I reply. "A warm breakfast sounds rejuvenating."

"Emily," she repeats. "Please...stay."

The expressions, *too good to be true*, and, *something has to go wrong*, suddenly hold more substance. "Okay," I reply tearfully. "We will stay."

The dining room is filled with all the scents of breakfast, belly laughter, and the most beautiful sound of all...his voice. We gather to give thanks, to reflect, and to look forward.

I do not know what tomorrow will bring but I didn't know yesterday what today would bring. Today my beautiful Jennet and my husband—a boy back from the grave. I no longer fear tomorrow.

As plates are dispensed and milk poured, I glance past the grinning faces to the three windows just beyond the dining-table. *Too good to be true*. Perched on the pane sits the grinning raven. He eyes me playfully, as if taunting me while I glue my shattered world together.

"What are you looking at, beautiful?" Kaleb asks before kissing my cheek.

"Nothing, my dear. It is nothing."

The End

Acknowledgements

If you're reading this, thank you.

To my friend, Carissa Lynch—thank you for your support. Your inspiration means more to me than you know. Allison Boyer, I appreciate your sharp eye and encouraging words.

To my family, thank you for allowing me to chase my goals! I love you!

About the Author

Bradon Nave was born and raised in rural Oklahoma. He attended a small country school during junior high and high school, and graduated with only three people in his class. After graduate school, he decided to devote his spare time to his passion of writing. Bradon currently lives in Piedmont, Oklahoma, with his wife and two young children.

When he's not writing, he loves running, being with friends and family, and being outdoors.

Facebook:
http://www.facebook.com/bradonnavebooks

Twitter:
http://www.twitter.com/BradonNave

Website:
http://www.bradonnave.com/